BLOOD KIN

Cole Vallantry, outnumbered and cornered, desperately swinging punches, is about ready to concede defeat — and not only regarding the brawl in the Buscadero saloon. His mission, the manhunt which had dragged him across Arizona in the blazing midsummer, is at a standstill, the trail having finally petered out. Then a tall stranger wades into the fracas, unbelievably taking Vallantry's side — but what is *his* agenda?

Books by Ben Nicholas
in the Linford Western Library:

THIS MAN KILLS

BEN NICHOLAS

BLOOD KIN

Complete and Unabridged

LINFORD
Leicester

First published in Great Britain in 2006 by
Robert Hale Limited
London

First Linford Edition
published 2006
by arrangement with
Robert Hale Limited
London

The moral right of the author has been asserted

British Library CIP Data

Nicholas, Ben
    Blood kin.—Large print ed.—
    Linford western library
    1. Western stories
    2. Large type books
    I. Title
    823.9'2 [F]

    ISBN 1–84617–509–7

Published by
F. A. Thorpe (Publishing)
Anstey, Leicestershire

Set by Words & Graphics Ltd.
Anstey, Leicestershire
Printed and bound in Great Britain by
T. J. International Ltd., Padstow, Cornwall

This book is printed on acid-free paper

1

Rough Night in Buscadero

The first wild swinger bearing in on him proved easy pickings for Cole Vallantry. He belted the brawler unconscious with just one clean punch. As the saloon shook to the reverberations of two hundred pounds of doorman measuring his length on the floor, another of Finnerty's bruisers reached the besieged loner and brought a clubbed fist down on the back of his neck.

Vallantry's head rang like a gong. Although handy with his fists, the flashy newcomer to Buscadero was more boxer than brawler who preferred a one-to-one contest to a wild rough house like this any day of the week.

But here he had no choice. He'd started it, he would have to finish it — their way.

He realized the rabbit-killer punch had done him more good than harm. It cleared the whiskey fumes from his head that had been slowing him down. Suddenly he was ducking and weaving with all the old nimbleness of foot and keenness of eye and his footwork was remarkable as he easily eluded the angry men trying to crowd him into a corner, drinkers and scantily-garbed percenters wisely jumping out of their way.

He punched a red and hairy face then gagged as knuckles found his ribs. He ducked aside from a whistling hook and kicked the man in the crotch with all his strength. Chairs splintered and tables went over with bottles and glasses crashing to the floor as the three doormen left standing came after, spurred on by Finnerty's screams of rage from well in the background.

Finnerty was the shrunken gnome of a proprietor of the dingy dive who was sore at Vallantry, firstly for flirting with his woman and secondly for asking probing questions about an acquaintance.

Cole Vallantry would have liked to get at the little runt and land just one king hit on him, but didn't fancy his chances of getting to do that as he suddenly found himself staring at the floorboards from a distance of mere inches!

He hadn't even seen the blow that felled him. He couldn't believe he was down. Then the pain rushed in. A boot slammed his ribs and he twisted frantically this way, desperately the next.

Simple self-preservation saw him propel himself back onto his feet where he was quick to land a kick in the crotch and barely duck under the trajectory of a flung bottle that whacked the wall behind him and shattered, drenching two squealing percenters with watered whiskey.

He vaulted the bar and began pelting his attackers with Finnerty's bottled supplies, almost enjoying himself now but not about to hand himself any plaudits for overall effort.

In those hectic moments he found himself finally forced to concede he'd been doing a lousy job of tracking down the man with the huge bounty on his head here in Utah Territory. And in the situation he found himself moments later — about as undignified as it could get for a vain man as he was forced to duck beneath the bar flap and scuttle towards the side door beneath a fusillade of hurled objects — he was for the first time about ready to concede failure.

Was he losing his touch?

Barely had the bitter question posited in his mind before he was felled a second time inside a minute. Spitting blood and sawdust he rolled aside as a boot lashed at him again. He seized it and twisted viciously. There was a splintering crack of bone followed by a howl of pure agony as the foot went limp in his grasp.

The crippled brawler had passed out.

The blood-curdling howling from the injured man on the floor saw the semi-circle of saloon muscle hold back momentarily, realizing just how serious this was getting.

Vallantry seized the advantage and struggled up to one knee behind the cover of an upturned table then lunged for the batwings. His chest was afire, his breathing labored, there was a ringing in his ears. He was unashamedly on the run until two husky shapes loomed before him.

He snatched up a chair and splintered it against a craggy face. Blood sprayed and the doorman went down like a typhus case. Vallantry didn't see him fall. The remorseless throttle grip of the surviving man's sinewy arm was locked across his throat from behind and he was being bent backwards, boots lifting from the floor, kicking, powerless.

He remembered wondering if rat-faced Finnerty might go so far as to let them kill him? The bastard was from

Killarney. The Irish were capable of anything.

Then the voice sounded at his shoulder.

'Mind if I horn in on your dust-up, partner? You look like you could use a bit of a hand.'

He attempted to screw his head round to catch a glimpse of the owner of the voice, but the man holding him gave his imprisoned neck such a jerk that he almost blacked out from lack of oxygen.

The next sound he heard was that of a brutal punch connecting directly behind his head. Instantly the hammer-lock was broken and he heard a body hit the floor like a sack of trash.

But a sideways glance offered a blurred impression of a bronzed face, stalwart body and two bony-knuckled fists cocking like cannon as Finnerty threw his reserves into the fray.

The newcomer ducked under the first wild swing and drove his shoulder squarely into the man's chest. The doorman crashed backwards over the unconscious figure on the floor and didn't even kick.

A fast-reviving Vallantry seized an enemy by his apron and jerked him off balance, enabling the stranger to punch him twice in the head and send him flying over a table.

Suddenly Vallantry realized there was nobody left to hit. Finnerty had fled to the safety of the stairs, from which safe point he screamed orders to what was left of his bouncers. Two of these were still on their feet, but though they cursed and shook their fists they held back, likewise keeping well out of range.

Spitting blood, Vallantry clutched weakly at a powerful shoulder. 'Let's get the hell out of here, cowboy. I always believed in quitting the game while ahead. After you!'

But the stranger didn't move. Suddenly he was gaping at Vallantry wide-eyed and disbelieving, almost as if he was confronting a ghost.

'Goddamnit!' Vallantry hissed as

Finnerty's howls reached a new crescendo. 'Are you coming or do I leave
you here to get — '

The spell was broken.

'OK, OK,' the stranger panted and,
spinning on cowboy high heels, led the
way for the batwings.

Vallantry beat him outside. He
enjoyed a good ruckus as much as the
next man but had had his fill for one
night, and then some.

Finnerty's dimming screeching followed them out: 'Cut out their livers
and dish 'em up for me supper. One
hundred American dollars to the man
who cuts 'em down . . . both of 'em. No
questions asked . . . '

The voice died in their wake as the
two tall men strode away down the
shadow-haunted street. The batwings of
the saloon remained motionless behind
them. Finnerty could have offered the
world for their destruction at that
moment without drawing any further
takers. At that moment, the scene they
were leaving behind more closely

resembled a medical clearing station in the war between the states than a saloon.

The sudden cold night air hit Vallantry like a club. He would have fallen had not the other grabbed his arm. He was amazed at the strength of those lean fingers as they turned a corner and halted abruptly. Breathing hard and still clutching his arm, his rescuer now stared at him again in the same piercing way he'd done at the saloon.

'What are you called, pilgrim?' he demanded.

'Huh?' Vallantry could barely see straight. He didn't want conversation. All he wanted was to put a further two blocks between them and the saloon, followed by a double rye and a cheroot, in that order.

Irritated, he attempted to break free but was held in a vice. The man might really be a blacksmith. Surely only a smith could boast such strength.

'Damn you, leave me go or I'll — '

The fingers tightened their grip and blue eyes drilled into his own. 'Name. You owe me that for saving your ass, pilgrim.'

'All right, damn you.' Vallantry inhaled deeply. For a moment he was tempted to offer one of the aliases he was frequently forced to use in his unusual line of work, but decided almost defiantly to go with the truth. 'Cole Vallantry. Now can we . . . '

At last the hand dropped from his arm. He couldn't read the big man's expression in the gloom, but the voice he heard seemed choked with emotion as he breathed, 'B'God and by glory! I knew I reckernized you even after ten-twelve year or more. Cole, don't you know your own kid brother?'

Cole Vallantry went still. He was a hard man to shock or surprise but suddenly he was both.

After a long moment it seemed some hidden cord of memory stirred, and he heard himself whisper, 'Buck?' He held his hand knee-high. 'Li'l Buck . . . from

Frogtree Hollow?'

'Li'l Buck Vallantry — your brother!' The cowboy knuckled the corner of his eye. 'Doggone, if I wasn't so mad at you, Cole, I reckon I could bust out bawling.'

'Yeah, me too, I guess,' Cole Vallantry replied as he found himself suddenly taken in a massive bear hug. But if this loner had ever wept in his life it was too far back to remember.

★   ★   ★

Momma Pearl was puzzled. Having already heard the dramatic story of the long-lost brothers reuniting by chance right here in her town after fifteen long years apart, she'd been overjoyed when the flashy one, Cole, and the kid brother, Buck, had chosen her place to eat and sample her snake-eye whiskey, which she always served in cracked crockery cups.

Now she was disappointed.

A teak-tough little lady with eyes like

bullets and a vast knowledge of life, Momma had expected a whole lot more drama and emotion from the brothers Vallantry than they had offered thus far.

The blue-eyed cowboy boasted about the sunniest grin she'd ever seen, and was probably acting just about the way you'd expect, she conceded grudgingly. She supposed he at least appeared pretty emotional as he kept staring at his very unalike brother like he couldn't quite believe his luck — but the other one seemed more interested in her pickled hog jowls and snake-eye.

The older one was a handsome dog, she was prepared to concede as she studied him with a bright beady eye. But if Cole Vallantry was a genuinely happy and relaxed man right at that moment he was doing a fine job of concealing it.

The woman sniffed. Those handsome ones were all alike, she mused. Flashy, full of themselves and to hell with anybody else. Ever since he'd hit town some forty-eight hours earlier, this lean six-footer with the overlong hair and steely blue eyes that could turn a good woman's knees to water, had been either bordering on trouble or actually up to his neck in it.

From what she'd heard, he'd been within a whisper of taking the whipping he likely deserved up at Finnerty's when his cowboy brother from out of the past chimed in and tipped the scales in his favor.

Momma sniffed again. Having never bedded a genuinely handsome stud in her life, she was probably biased against the Cole Vallantry breed. And it didn't make her warm to him any to reflect on the fact that the ones who seemed to have looks, charm and personality served up to them on a platter, more often than not appeared destined to enjoy good fortune as well.

She'd give one of her few teeth to know what the heck the cowboy was laughing about now, and why the troublemaker was scowling back at him that way.

'So when Ma found out about the old man and the Cherokee squaw, she handed him a licking and his hat,' Buck Vallantry chuckled. 'That was seven years back come Thomas Jefferson Day. There's a rumor pa got caught under the blankets with the chief's wife on the reservation a couple of years later and wound up staked out on an ant's nest in the sun and his eyelids cut off.' He shook his head. 'That pa . . . eh?'

'Yeah, just what I was thinking. That pa!'

Cole Vallantry had spent remarkably little time over the past fifteen years thinking about his father, or any of the brood for that matter. This might have been attributable to some defect within himself. More likely, it stemmed from the fact that from the very start this man had fervently believed he'd been accidentally born into a third-grade family by some cosmic mistake, and that the smartest move he'd ever made in life was to abandon the whole cracker bunch of them the day he was old enough.

He cared nothing about his pa or his fate, real or mythical. Or any of them, if he was to be brutally honest. Which was why he found himself vaguely puzzled about what he was doing seated here waiting for their whiskey and the greasy chili and grits, instead of putting long miles between himself and the man seated opposite.

He took time out to grab a moment for some deep thinking. Finally he found himself nodding slowly to himself. Understanding was finally coming clearer, brushing aside the fogs of hoopla clouding this reunion. For the longer he studied his brother and assessed his mooted skills as horse-breaker, trailsman and gun cowboy, the more he was forced to acknowledge that Buck might just prove out to be more of an asset than the liability he'd initially taken him for.

'What you dreaming about, bro?'

'Huh?' Cole blinked and frowned. 'Er, nothing special.'

They paused as Momma's cute little daughter brought the vittles to the table. The girl was about the only halfway attractive feature of Buscadero's counter-and-stool eating house at the wagon yard end of the main street. It was advertised as an eating house but smelled like wildcat whiskey. In the burgeoning territory, where government marshals battled to limit the mischief of the bootleggers, such places were known as blind pigs.

Cole hated blind pigs and wildcat whiskey. He had highly cultivated tastes, but catering for them had been an increasingly difficult task of late.

The longer he worked on what was shaping up as the biggest job of his life, the farther he seemed to drift from success. And not for the first time tonight, the back of his mind posed the query: was the job simply too big for one man?

'Dime for your thoughts, brother.'

Cole blinked.

'You'd be paying too much — brother,

believe me. Tell me, where are you headed?'

Buck made a sweeping gesture that embraced the entire southwest.

'Rogue River first up. I go down across the river and up into the high mesa country around this time every year rounding up and breaking the mustangs there. Something I started a few years back, and now I've got my own horse ranch in Cascade County.' He grinned. 'Did I chance to tell you I bust horses real good?'

Cole didn't even hear. His brain was racing. His secret destination was Placerville. He didn't know much about that big town as yet but did know it was situated on the Rogue, the deep-water river that brought life and commerce to the entire Eagle County region of southwestern Utah.

Placerville, Eagle County, and a man named Singleman. Rolling the names on his tongue he could almost taste the danger. A man could get killed down there, even a survivor like him.

Again he focused on the man seated

opposite. He'd viewed his brother as a reincarnation of the old man at first glance, but maybe that was being too harsh. He was beginning to detect signs of a keen native intelligence behind the laconic manner and maybe more than just a suggestion of worldly-wide shrewdness. Buck had already shown he could use his hands like sledge-hammers, and he'd noted before that he wore a sixgun like someone who might just know how to use one.

So . . . just where the hell was his thinking leading him?

A shadow fell through Momma Pearl's street door. A deputy stood there, lean, lank and chewing a cud of black shag-cut tobacco. His mean yellow eyes played over the room until they came to rest on the brothers. He beckoned imperiously. Cole was about to give him the finger when the glint of sunlight on metal from the street caught his eye. He realized the town sheriff was standing out by the hitchrail with a sawed-off cradled in the crook of his arm.

Cole had been in town long enough to know the lawman was dyspeptic, probably alcoholic and tough as old bootheels. And right now in the aftermath of the big dust-up at Finnerty's, the man looked sore as a boil.

'Looks like we've stepped on someone's corns,' he growled, rising. 'But if this hick badgepacker thinks he can push Cole Vallantry around — '

'Take it easy,' counseled Buck, also getting up. 'Always look for the easy way out before you bite down on the hard.' He winked. 'Bit of homespun advice from the old man.'

'That the same old man who looked for and found the easy way out all his no-account life?' He silenced the other's protest with a gesture. 'Come on, see what he wants. But I've had a tough day, he'd better realize. I'm burning on what you might call a short fuse.'

Not as short as the lawman's, it seemed.

The two weren't rightly out the door before the sheriff started in on them.

He had with him a damages bill from the saloon. There were men with serious injuries, they were told. Who the hell did they think they were — drifting into a law-abiding town and turning it into a battleground. The fine was twenty dollars apiece or they could talk things over with the justice of the peace in the morning after a night at the jailhouse.

Cole called him a dirty name. The sawed-off jerked up and the hammer cocked. The sheriff showed the weapon to Cole but somehow Buck managed to insert himself between the two. Gently he took hold of the barrel and fingered it aside, his grin like sunshine.

'Sheriff McCauley, ain't it, sir?' His tone was respectful. He nodded. 'Yeah, that's your handle right enough. Known clear across the country and all the ways up into the dusty hills country along the border as just about the finest frontier lawman in this part of Utah.' A pause to grin again. 'Sure hope that don't sound too sugary, Sheriff, but it ain't every day a wandering cowboy gets to meet up with a genuine legend of the law, that's for sure.'

Cole eased back a pace and rested hand on gunbutt. This sounded so much like pure horsecrap to him that he was certain the sheriff would recognize it as such and react accordingly.

Instead, McCauley lowered his weapon and frowned in puzzlement. 'Finnerty told me you was the one that done the most damage . . . and that I'd likely need a posse to take you in.' A pause. 'You don't look like any kind of hell-raising rafter-rattler to me, son. What say you, Deputy?'

The deputy turned his head and spat. He thought Buck looked and sounded like a man who'd learned how to turn bullcrap into a science. But no deputy badgeman disagreed with McCauley unless he was keen to swell the ranks of the unemployed.

'Mebbe Finnerty got it wrong, Shurf.'

21

'I gotta allow those boys at the saloon were acting a mite inhospitable towards my brother when I happened by, Sheriff,' Buck weighed in. 'And that ain't exactly fair.' He gestured at a bemused Cole. 'Guess you wouldn't know by looking at him that my brother's been sickly and kinda poorly all his life, now would you, sir? Mystery illness Doc Peach from back home called it. Makes him weak with a feeling he could die any minute, and you can see how feeling that way all the time could turn a man kinda sour on life and make him a tad difficult to get along with. A man of the world like you would understand that, I figure?'

At that point Cole Vallantry removed hand from gunbutt and simply stood back in silence to watch McCauley slowly transform from trouble-hunting badgeman to putty in his brother's leathery palms in just a matter of moments.

It ended up with handshakes all round and no fines imposed before the brothers were allowed to make off along Main, free as jaybirds.

Buck looked pleased with himself, but his brother was silent and thoughtful as he worked his way toward a major decision.

He studied the man at his side for half a block, then halted abruptly and made his proposition. Seeing as both were heading in the same general direction, maybe Buck might like to tag along?

It was like taking candy from a kid, he reflected later. Agreeing like a shot, Buck Vallantry acted like the opportunity to team up with his long-gone oldest brother after all those years was about the best thing that had ever happened to anybody.

'Good man,' Cole applauded as they clasped hands. He winked. 'Or at least the best since you heard the old man had likely been scalped, gelded, pegged out and left to the ants, huh?'

Buck's smile faded at that, yet he forced it back into place. He reckoned it only natural that it might take some time for him to get used to his brother's weird sense of humor after all those years apart.

★ ★ ★

Cole Vallantry's conscience was crystal clear as he rode up out of the sandy wash and reined in beneath the thrown shade of a lonesome liveoak and waited for his brother to catch up.

The fact that he had quit the family home in Arkansas fifteen years earlier and never returned was something he'd always been proud of, rather than ashamed and guilty as he sensed Buck half-expected him to be.

He grinned slyly in the shadow of his low-tugged hat. Had he ever been that innocent and naïve? He smiled with wry amusement as he lighted up a cigar and watched the smoke drift away sluggishly in the still heat of day.

Horse and rider looking twelve-feet high in the glaring sunlight of the valley lands, Buck Vallantry loomed into sight behind and headed steadily toward him, having fallen back earlier to remove a stone from his horse's foot.

Cole shook his head in wonder. Mounted and at a distance, Buck was a physical replica of the old man. The resemblance was uncanny.

There were seven siblings in the family and from his earliest days Cole had rated himself as the only one with the ambition, brains and style to guarantee success in the wider world beyond Frogtree Hollow.

At fifteen he secured a job as water boy on a wagon train and had never returned. He subsequently spent four years in the southern gray of the Confederacy and had been living an increasingly exciting, dangerous and selfish life ever since.

'Sure we're on the right trail?' he grunted, swigging from his canteen.

'I ain't never wrong about directions,' came the confident reply. Buck rubbed his horse's sweating muzzle. 'Or critters

25

neither. Yessir, guess I'm kind of an expert on those kinda things.' He squinted against the glare. 'So, what's your speciality, Cole? You ain't exactly said.'

Cole considered lying, but decided it might be high time to start opening up little by little in order to minimize the shock for Buck when he finally discovered the full truth about him and how he made his living.

'What do you think of manhunting for a trade?' he asked casually.

Buck blinked. 'Manhunter? You saying that what you are? Hey, you ain't saying that you're a dirty — ?

'Bounty hunter?' Cole anticipated. He shook his head and smiled reassuringly. 'No way. That's about as low as a man can get. But you'd agree that seeking out criminals and killers for the federal government and the president is a very different proposition?'

'I guess . . . ' Buck didn't sound quite sure. 'Is that what your business is, Cole? You're tailing somebody for the government?'

He nodded.

'One of the worst ever — killer, traitor, fugitive. You name it and Singleman's done it, is it and will one day have to pay for it.'

'Singleman's his name then?'

'Big Nick Singleman. Ever heard of him?'

'Guess not.'

'You will if you stick with me. And you are sticking with me, aren't you, brother? For a spell, at least. I could use a good sidekick right now.'

Buck didn't respond immediately. For a brief moment, feeling those blue eyes probing at him, Cole Vallantry feared he might have underestimated the other. That maybe Buck was far sharper than he chose to reveal.

He hoped he was wrong, and after a moment it seemed that was the case.

'Well, if you put it that way, mebbe I could give you a little time and help out some.' Buck responded, swatting a horsefly with lethal accuracy. 'You ready to dust?'

'Never readier . . . brother.'

They mounted and set the southwest between their horses' ears. Buck calculated it to be less than fifty miles to the big river.

2

Big River, Big Men

The moon was rising as the two men made their way down to the levee.

Before them, wide, swift and deep lay the Rogue. By day the river carried downstream the trash of five counties, but Lady Night had transformed her magically into a smooth flowing band of silver and gold. Yet all that concerned the pair standing silhouetted against the moon, one tall and the other broad, was not the beauty of the scene but rather just how swiftly the waters were flowing.

'Running strong, boss,' the hatchet-faced man observed, gazing up-river where the paddle-wheeler Dixie Belle would appear next morning. 'She should tie up early. About eleven tomorrow would be my guess.'

The big man fingered his gold watch-chain strung across his waistcoat, rubbed large hands briskly together. 'Fine, now that everything's clicking into place, Hatch, I'll find my own way home while you stick with the boat and the colonel. I'd stay on here and oversee the operation but there are too many demands on my time back at Rivertown. Everything clear with you?'

'Sure, boss,' grunted Casey Hatch. 'I understand.' He understood right enough. Singleman was pleading pressures of business as the reason he was leaving to overland his way back to his down-river headquarters out of Rivertown. But Hatch understood the true reason behind the big man's decision. The planned kidnapping of possibly the most powerful citizen from northern Steuben County would raise all kinds of hell all over. If anything should go amiss with the operation, the big man planned to be long gone leaving lesser men to take the rap.

'Any last queries?' Singleman snapped.

30

Hatch rubbed his heavy jaw. 'Well, now that you mention it . . . '

'What?'

'Well, you know this Reece geezer you brought in to keep tabs on Palmer? Well, he's done a good job, I'll allow. But the varmint drinks too free and tends to get real talky on the gin . . . if you know what I mean?'

'You're saying he could prove a risk now?' the big man asked sharply.

'Could be. And I know you hate taking chances, boss man.'

'In that case, seeing as he's already completed his part of the job, the solution's simple.'

'It is?'

'Kill him.'

'Huh? Do you mean it?' Hatch paused, then finally nodded as he understood. 'Reckon you do at that, boss.'

'You'll be well paid. Anything else?'

'Ah . . . I guess not.'

'Then I'll see you at Rivertown. Good luck.'

31

Big Nick moved lightly for a man his size as he strode off smartly to where surrey and driver waited in the shadows of the long dockside warehouse. Watching the handsome rig receding through intermittent patches of feeble light, Casey Hatch, in a rare moment of reflection, mused that Singleman seemed to have been designed by nature as a creature of the shadows. A man rarely saw his face in the sunlight; he could come and go like whisper, no small feat for a man of over two hundred pounds.

He turned his stare to the river that was carrying a prominent Steuben County power-broker, rancher, militia leader and local hero ever closer to Placerville with every passing minute.

When the rubber-tyred surrey was finally gone from sight the cat-footed hellion massaged his gaunt and ravaged face and made off towards the lights of the levee town with a purposeful stride. An hour later the body of Joe Reece was floating downstream, facedown in the river. Casey Hatch was skilled at many things, but at murder he was better than most.

★　★　★

They were drawing close to the river country although nothing about the land they crossed hinted at that yet. This final stretch of arid country was still a hell in bad weather, and frustration was starting to wear Cole Vallantry thin by the time he reined in to enjoy the protection of a solitary saguaro cactus rearing twenty feet above him into the bleached out sky.

Something struck his shoulder. It was a chewed up chunk of cactus flesh. He stared up to see the woodpecker working on a hole in the cactus, foam and pulp spewing from its busy beak.

Somehow all the raw harshness of the country seemed encapsulated in this image for the manhunter who, despite his wide experience in the harsher places of the West, was still at heart what he'd always been, a dandy with a taste for the good things of life — those good things for which he seemed to find himself working harder and more dangerously to acquire as he moved towards the big thirty-fifth birthday — the halfway mark.

He hipped around in the saddle, reflected light from his bola clasp glinting upwards along his lean jawline.

His scowl deepened as he focused on the approaching silhouette of his brother astride his mean-eyed Sioux stallion.

It might have been the weather, or it could have been something as simple as the fact that Cole Vallantry was beginning to realize he'd in some ways misjudged his newly found kinsman, that caused his momentary unease.

In his naïveté, he'd hoped Buck would prove to be the lucky break he'd been searching for ever since taking on a potentially lethal job that nobody else seemed to want, namely the bringing down of a shadowy criminal currently occupying the number three rating on the Coloradan provincial marshals' most wanted list, Big Nick Singleman.

It had seemed the kid brother was emerging even more of a bargain on the trails than he might have hoped for just a couple of days back. But other characteristics had emerged along the trail, unwelcome traits of personality and perceptions from Cole Vallantry's point of view.

Buck had a big contract with a major horse-broker to hunt and break as many wild horses as he could rope in at Satchequaw Hills some fifty miles beyond Rogue River, so he'd learned. If he rounded up and broke to saddle and bridle enough quality wild stuff without breaking his neck, his brother stood to make a fair piece of money out of the operation.

Cole's interest in running himself ragged chasing mustangs that had rarely sighted a human being, much less ones with ropes bent on snaring them and breaking them into saddle and bridle, hovered at around zero.

By contrast, he himself personally

was confronting a challenge infinitely more dangerous than any mustang hunt could ever be, where, although the risks were fearsome, the rewards were high. In addition, a man in his position wouldn't be called upon to shovel any horse shit and had good prospects of wearing a clean-boiled shirt every day and dining off quality plate at night, important attractions for a man of his tastes and vanities.

But the bottom line was that Cole Vallantry badly needed a reliable sidekick and was already convinced Buck filled that bill. He'd imagined it would prove simple to talk the big man around, what with the kid being so excited and fired up about their finding one another and all the rest of that sentimental buffalo dust that seemed so important to him and all.

It wasn't quite working that way.

Even if the seemingly highly moral young Buck believed his brother was working legitimately on special assignment for the marshals over in Colorado government as he'd been assured, the young cowboy hadn't shown even a flicker of interest when told about some shadowy figure named Singleman.

Maybe had Cole risked adding the information that Singleman was worth $5,000 dead or alive back north, his brother might have shown more interest, although he doubted it. For a confident man handy with the fists and likely slick with a gun, Buck Vallantry seemed genuine to his brother's experienced eye.

Even worse, Buck was now in turn pressing Cole to join up him in the Satchequaws for a summer of hard work, high excitement and the rare pleasure of honest money earned and the satisfaction of a job well done at the conclusion of it all.

The man must be loco!

He thoughtfully drew one of the last of his fine cigars from his breast pocket. He wasn't about to either quit his assignment or risk busting up their fraternal partnership. A tough operator lived behind the thirty dollar shirts and fifty dollar boots of Spanish leather.

If he couldn't talk a country 'hick' around, then he reckoned he didn't belong in the business he was in — a 'business' that, not too long ago, he would have considered far beneath him.

'I can smell the Rogue,' he remarked as Buck joined him and reined in. He could do no such thing, but it was a pleasant image to toy with. 'Soon we'll be sailing along that broad-bosomed river on our way to Rivertown in a luxury paddle-wheeler and, if my tip is worth a dime and if we're as good at smelling out skunks as I reckon we are, Singleman and a five thousand dollar reward should be ours to share in jig time. What say you, brother?'

'Let's keep riding.'

'We can ride and talk at the same time, you know.'

'I'm willing to talk,' Buck grinned, pushing his horse ahead, 'providing we talk only about chitlings.'

'Chitlings?'

'As I recollect, you were always right partial to a big platter of chitlings way back when, brother.'

Cole Vallantry's stare drilled bullet hard at his brother's back. Was it possible that this reincarnation of the old man was trying to cut him down a peg or two by constantly reminding him of their humble beginnings? Was he sharp enough to do that?

'As I recall,' he retorted testily, 'when you were just a tad and you got too damn noisy — way back when — I used to flick the back of your ears, mister.'

'You could likely still do that, brother,' came the easy response. 'On one condition.'

'And what might that be?'

Buck glanced back at him over his shoulder. 'Why, that you got your affairs in order first, of course.'

Cole waited for the grin to follow. It didn't show. He felt himself flush. The hick horse-breaker was actually bracing him!

For a moment Cole Vallantry's temper flashed, then as quickly subsided. He told himself the time might well come he would have to take 'the kid' aside and teach him a little respect. But not yet. When a man played for big stakes, whether at the tables or in the lethal profession he currently followed, he must learn to ignore the pin-pricks and focus on the main game. In the game he expected to begin unfolding ahead of him down at the river town of Placerville, he was likely to find himself with more on his plate to worry about than pin-pricks coming from mouthy kid brothers.

He told himself he felt calm and assured as the weak sun squinted from behind clouds and the hoof-lifted dust fogged behind them, yet he still felt the need to light up one of his last cigars.

He calculated they would raise the river by nightfall.

★ ★ ★

Slick Donovan raked in the pot with practiced skill. It contained almost forty dollars and most of it previously belonging to the colonel. Not any longer. The gambler stared at Nathan Palmer with glittering black eyes.

'Another hand, Colonel?'

'Of course, sir. You don't seriously think I'd be deterred by such a piffling loss, do you?'

Colonel Nathan Palmer was by far the most distinguished of all the paddle-wheeler's well-heeled passengers chancing their luck in the Dixie Belle's gambling salon that night. With his fine silver hair, mustache and courtly manners, the former wartime militia hero was ruddy, upstanding, self-assured — and running low on cash. But he certainly wasn't to be intimidated by an incredibly unlucky run at poker.

'Honestly, father,' protested the fair-haired young woman at this side as she rose from her plush chair, 'you've been playing for hours. You really must rest.'

'We didn't rest at Bull Run or Gettysburg, m'dear,' he told his daughter with a chuckle. 'Nor shall we run from this gentleman's uncanny luck. Deal the cards if you will, sir.'

'But, father — '

'Let's play cards, gentlemen,' Donovan snapped with a hard look at the girl. Then he forced an oily grin. 'Your father's luck is bound to change, missy.'

Lauren Palmer shrugged resignedly as the six players pushed their stakes into the center of the baize-colored table. She loved her father but knew he could be a fool at gambling, amongst other things she'd sooner not mention. He really should know better than play with total strangers.

The cards went flashing around the table beneath the green-shaded droplight.

The colonel won a small pot and the fat Arizona cattle baron drew four aces but ruined his prospects of building up a big center by betting too high in his excitement and scaring everybody out of the hand.

Donovan winked across at the frowning girl and dealt another hand.

The longer the game continued the more the colonel lost. He tried bluff, switched to playing conservatively, even thought once or twice of quitting the game and enduring the subsequent loss of face.

But the man was an inveterate gambler. Even his enemies knew that.

The strains of 'The Blue Danube' played upon a harpsichord seeped through from the adjacent parlor room. Water lapped gently against the ship's sturdy hull. More people crowded in and most collected around the poker layout where the colonel had now decided to bet big as his latest stratagem.

Slick Donovan won that hand and the next. Lauren Palmer couldn't watch any longer and was drifting towards the porthole when she noticed the young man enter from the main companionway.

She paused to stare. It wasn't so much the undeniable fact that the newcomer was both strikingly handsome and athletic looking that captured her attention; he simply appeared so clean, sunbronzed and healthy compared with the fat, middle-aged passengers and the slick-haired dealers and hangers-on surrounding that it caused him to stand out.

Moments later, when he cocked his head at a certain angle, she realized she knew him.

He was spruced up in a clean shirt and Levis, and she hoped he might glance her way. Instead he stood staring at the poker players, frowning at first, then breaking into a big white grin.

'Well, howdy do there, Colonel Palmer sir!' he exclaimed.

Everyone turned. Palmer tossed down another worthless hand and swivelled round in his chair. He stared, then jumped to his feet.

'Well, young Buck Vallantry, as I live and breathe!'

The men shook hands warmly and patted one another on the shoulder, the salon watching with interest. The onlookers soon realized from what was said that Colonel Palmer and one Buck Vallantry had spent time together hunting buffalo on the Kree Plains two years earlier, Vallantry filling the role of head scout while the colonel footed the bills.

'A drink for the finest scout on the plains!' Palmer called to the bar, then was politely thrust aside by the young woman in the pale pink gown.

'Buck Vallantry,' she smiled. 'Don't you remember me?'

Vallantry stared blankly at the slender figure for a moment before his eyes brightened with recognition.

'Miss Lauren! But it can't be you. You were only knee high to a —'

'I was eighteen and now I'm twenty,' she interrupted. Then she smiled. 'But it is very nice to see you again, Buck Vallantry. Are you booked aboard the Dixie Belle?'

'I sure am, but — '

'The game, gentlemen?' a sour voice prompted.

Donovan stood impatiently by his chair shuffling the deck of cards. 'In or out, Colonel?'

The colonel was in. The girl immediately showed concern. Vallantry noticed, and asked if anything was amiss.

'Just about everything, Buck,' she confessed, and as an old acquaintance, proceeded to confide in him concerning the colonel's recklessness and subsequent losses. 'He really should never gamble, as you most probably recall from our safari days on the high plains. He does just about everything so well, all but gambling. And to tell you the truth,' she added, lowering her voice, 'I'm sure the dealer is feeding other players — probably his stooges — top cards so that Father just loses and loses . . . '

Vallantry frowned as he moved closer to study the layout. He'd come in for a shot after checking in, but that could wait. He didn't rate himself as a gambling expert yet by the same token was no rube either. After just minutes following the run of play he was convinced the girl was right in her suspicions.

He watched eight hands being played out. The colonel lost seven times. By his yardstick, the arithmetic involved in that sort of outcome simply didn't add up. He was half-tempted to take mean-eyed Donovan by the scruff and throw him over the side, but then had a better notion.

There was another way to handle this.

He turned away from the girl. 'Excuse me, Miss Lauren. Got to go see a feller.'

★   ★   ★

Cole Vallantry sipped brandy and soaked his aching feet.

His last information, from a certain semi-legitimate source with intelligence

47

spies embedded with Headquarters, had hardened the suspicion that the elusive Singleman was possibly lying low someplace in the Rivertown region downstream from Placerville. Additional detail — sketchy as was all such on the crime boss — suggested that from time to time it was believed the man with the big money on his head had been sighted at upstream Placerville itself.

As a consequence of that tip Cole had set off afoot to comb the sprawling riverside town end to end, hoping to get lucky early. This had taken the better part of three hours without result. As a consequence he now felt bushed and frustrated as he poured himself another jolt.

His frustration stemmed from the fact that although he'd not caught even a whiff of his quarry, he had picked up hints and whispers suggesting that Singleman might well have been within the vicinity of Placerville itself quite recently.

Could be he'd just missed him, the sonuva!

But wasn't that the story of every manhunter, legitimate or otherwise, who took on the task of tracking that one down? The almost, the close miss?

As always Cole hated to be bundled in with the mob.

Yet a man could scarcely argue with a lack of success, he brooded. And wondered if maybe he wasn't up to the job after all . . . ?

Although still rated at only number three on the most wanted list over in western Colorado, Singleman could boast by far the highest bounty on his head. The reason for this was that the authorities regarded his cleverness, agenda and criminal potential far greater than the two above him who commanded higher rewards based simply upon the number of atrocities committed.

Singleman of course also killed. But what distinguished him from the bank robbers and high-grade con men of the territory was that he had been, and could easily be again, a potential danger to the political structure and the very balance of power up north in the Steuben County region of Utah Territory. Singleman was alleged to have been involved in attempted coups, political assassinations, bribery, corruption and coercion at high levels. It was mainly due to the power and influence he still wielded in Steuben County, despite having been recently confronted and driven out of the region by Colonel Palmer's free-riding militiamen. Authorities in two territories feared Singleman could return to a position of power in the north if not apprehended, hence the impressive size of the bounty on his head.

Cole understood that Colorado had a chance of making certain charges against a power manipulator stick, whereas his native Utah probably did not. If not reigned in or eliminated, there could be no accurate prediction of how far Singleman might go were he to return to his power base in remote and poorly governed Steuben County, which politician experts seemed to believe could be quite on the cards.

That sort of threat was guaranteed to focus the minds of governments and the law. The hunt for Singleman had thus far defied both the undermanned army and the widely scattered law agencies across the territory.

Singleman remained very much at large and operative.

Cole Vallantry was just one hunter committed to locating the man. But far from being in any way connected to the law, judiciary or army, he was his own man committed to winning where others had failed, any way he saw fit and using any methods to achieve success.

It suited him at times to affect connections with legitimate law. But he was well outside that spectrum and that was his secret. Headquarters, the agency he worked for currently in Colorado, had no legitimate status but was a bounty operation, pure and unadorned.

He got up and moved to the porthole of the state-room he occupied. Couples and families were moving leisurely about the levees and jetties in the early evening, the first lights beginning to blink on. He wanted another shot but decided against it. His day wasn't over yet, and when you camped on the trail of a criminal of Singleman's caliber a man couldn't risk getting drunk and maybe ending up beneath the Dixie Belle instead of aboard her.

The door opened without a knock and his brother strode in. Cole wondered where Buck got his energy. Maybe it was the clean living. Compared to his hard-living oldest brother, beer-and-beefsteak Buck lived a pretty clean life.

'What?' he growled. He wanted to be out there amongst all those pretty women on board, was peeved because his assignment kept taking precedence.

Buck told him. He'd bumped into Colonel Palmer, one of Utah's finest and an old friend from the high plains.

He'd come to inform his brother that he had reason to believe the colonel was at that moment being taken to the cleaners by a salon card sharp.

'So?'

'So, you told me you're a nonesuch wonder with the pasteboards. How about getting your boots on and coming on down to the salon and show this card slick some of your tricks and help get the colonel's money back.'

'No.'

'What do you mean . . . no? This man was a hero in the war and — '

'And has to be six kinds of a fool to let himself get taken down by the kind of shifty characters that everyone knows prey on the riverboats.'

'But, Cole — '

'No buts,' he grouched, going back to the brandy bottle. 'I'm on a big assignment that's taking up all my time and energy. Go tell your colonel he can go — '

'He's got a pretty daughter.'

'So?'

'Just figured you might be interested.'

'How pretty?'

'As a field of Texas bluebonnets.'

'Fetch me my boots.'

3

The Colonel is Missing

The cards had been shaved.

Cole Vallantry's highly skilled fingers told him this before he'd been sitting in on the big game five minutes. He tossed in his hand and leaned back to draw a silver cigar case from an inside pocket of his jacket and selected a cheroot that retailed at three for four dollars.

All watched him as he puffed blue smoke toward the chandelier above the poker table — the cattle baron from up-country, the salesman with hope in his eyes and very little in his billfold, the colonel appearing jovial and confident despite his losses, and prominent amongst the others, Slick Donovan.

Donovan was table boss and the big winner so far tonight. Tall, sleek-haired and ice-eyed, the man was assessing the new player with a professional eye as the travelling salesman dealt up another hand. Vallantry glanced the man's way, dropped his gaze to the slim, supple hands that were decorated by three signet rings.

Cole studied those nimble fingers as the cards went round and around and was ready to believe that Donovan could perform magic with pasteboards, particularly when they had been shaved in a variety of ways to identify suit and number. He'd detected that subtle fact almost from the outset.

The man to Donovan's right, a lumber dealer from across the border, cut the deck and put the halves together. Donovan picked up the deck and glanced at Vallantry.

'Jacks to open.'

'I'll try and remember,' Cole answered.

The cards flashed around the circular table. Cole picked up his hand. A pair of kings. Donovan was as obvious as a bull buffalo in a bathtub, he mused. He dealt out good cards first up to sucker the other players in before fiddling with his crooked deck. Vallantry opened for five dollars. The cattle buyer bumped it to ten and the colonel matched him. The other players dropped out. Slick Donovan fingered fifteen dollars into the center.

'Cost you ten to see,' he told the table.

He won that hand and the cards went round and round.

'Oh, Buck,' the girl whispered worriedly. 'Father is still losing, and your brother appears to be also.'

'Don't fret any, missy. Cole knows what he's doing.'

'Are you sure?'

He was sure. One night out on the trail, Cole had produced a deck of cards to kill time. In the space of a few minutes he'd shown his brother more slick and shifty tricks than he'd ever dreamed existed. True, Cole was down quite a sum by this. But his brother knew he was only suckering the cheating player in.

He hoped.

The fortunes of the game rose and fell as some won and others lost and dropped out until only three were left, Donovan, the colonel and Vallantry.

Now, Cole decided.

The cards went out. He studied his hand. Four kings. He placed the cards down, aware of Donovan's eye on him.

'Well, Vallantry?'

'Open.' He pushed a fifty into the center and a gasp rose from the onlookers. Up until that point, twenty dollars had been the top wager.

'Your fifty, Mr Vallantry,' said the perspiring colonel, 'and fifty more.'

Donovan suppressed a triumphant grin; this was what he'd been waiting for. 'Big pot,' he commented, feigning nervousness.

'Cost you a hundred,' Cole murmured.

'I'm in.'

'Raise you,' Vallantry murmured, and the colonel swore in disgust and flung down his cards. 'Too rich for this old soldier's blood, gentlemen. I've had enough.'

'I'm still in,' Donovan murmured, pushing notes into the center. He discarded three cards and Vallantry figured he was holding two aces and the next two cards he dealt himself — certain Vallantry would not discard — had to be two more aces. 'Cards, Mr Vallantry?'

Cole took his time responding. He knew he'd been deliberately dealt four kings, an almost unbeatable hand under normal circumstances.

'How many cards?' Donovan was growing impatient.

Vallantry tossed down three cards. Donovan turned white. He'd had it all figured to deal himself the extra two bullets and haul in the pot.

'Three cards?' He sounded hoarse. 'Are you sure?'

'I must be a lousy player, but yeah, three it is.'

A worried Lauren Palmer squeezed Buck's arm. He liked it.

'Oh, Buck, all that money and much of it Father's. Is that awful man going to take it?'

Cole was so expert at gambling deceit that even his brother was taken in. But Buck put on a brave face.

'Of course he'll win, girl. Can't you tell he's just playing with this sucker?'

Lauren studied Donovan again and had to admit that the sharp-featured dealer, now staring across at Cole over that big pile of cash, appeared a far cry from his formerly assured self.

The girl made to speak but Cole's voice reached them clearly.

'I'm waiting, Donovan. And on account of the size of the pot, I'm claiming any player's right to call for a finger deal.'

'What?'

Cole met Donovan's stare calmly. He had no intention of giving him the opportunity to deal himself a full hand of aces. He glanced around. 'I'm within my rights, gentlemen. Isn't that so?'

A chorus of affirmation rose around

the table. They knew their poker.

Donovan was desperate. His eyes took on the enamelled look of a snake's as he half rose from his chair.

'Damn you, I take this as a reflection on my honesty. I've a good mind to — '

Cole Vallantry reached out across the table, seized him by his string tie and drew his pale, sharp-featured face close to his own.

'Sit down and deal. Three cards for me and as many as you want, mister!'

The only sound to be heard was the sibilant splashing of the little waves against the Dixie Belle's smooth white hull as a sweating Donovan lowered his rump to his chair and picked up the pack.

'One finger,' Vallantry said with authority. 'Three cards.'

Numbly, Donovan pushed out the next three cards face down with his index finger, then like a man in a trance, gave himself three the same way. Vallantry studied his hand with a smile. He now held two kings, two aces and another.

He tossed the cards down carelessly, face-up.

'Let me guess, dealer,' he smiled. 'My pot?'

The cards tumbled from Donovan's hands. Necks craned all around the table. He had a pair of aces. The pot was Vallantry's.

He was reaching for the money when Donovan cursed wildly, kicked his chair back and reached for the bulge beneath his left armpit.

As his hand closed over gunbutt, a hand whipped over his shoulder and seized his forearm with fingers like steel. His face erupting with nervous sweat, Donovan glanced up to stare into the smiling bronzed face of the younger brother.

'Leave go of that shooter or you're going to have to get used to scratching one-handed,' Buck warned him amiably.

Slick Donovan let go of his gun.

⋆ ⋆ ⋆

'Absolutely not, gentlemen,' Colonel Palmer protested. 'Under no circumstances could I accept such a sum.'

'Sure you can,' Buck Vallantry insisted. He grinned across the colonel's stateroom at Cole standing lazily by the door, his relaxed manner in stark contrast to the toughness he'd shown a short time before in the players' room. 'You tell him, bro.'

'It's rightfully yours, Colonel,' Cole obliged. 'That snake stole most of it from you, only fitting you should get it back.'

'But some of it at least is yours . . .'

Now both brothers were shaking their heads in unison. The girl had given Buck some idea of how much her father had lost before enlisting their aid. Buck was happy to see the colonel take it all. Cole was less happy but enjoyed the good impression he knew he must be creating in pretty Lauren's mind by doing so.

'We're flush, actually,' he lied. Then he sobered. 'But learn a lesson from this, Colonel. To put it delicately, you're not as young as you used to be. It takes youth and nerves to play poker with strangers for big money.'

Colonel Nathan Palmer reached for the notes. He wasn't smiling now. Cole had struck a nerve. Although sixty-one years of age and senatorially silver-haired, Lauren's once famous father still looked in the mirror every morning and saw the rough-riding young Palmer of the civil war days. Any mention of age always had a negative effect on the colonel and he was suddenly distracted, thinking less about cash and card sharps and reminding himself there were other ways of perking up that old youthful feeling other than playing high-stake poker with strangers.

Buck walked to the door and opened it. As Cole put on his hat, Lauren impetuously stood on tiptoe and kissed his cheek.

'Thank you so much,' she said breathlessly. 'You were really quite wonderful.' She turned to Buck. 'As were you, Buck.' She planted a kiss flush on the surprised cowboy's mouth.

Buck grinned but Cole did not. A mere peck on the cheek for him — the hero of the hour — but the full smooch for his brother whose main contribution to their success had been brow-beating him into taking part in the affair?

Plainly, and despite her obvious class, Lauren Palmer had no taste whatever in that curvy body of hers . . .

'Both you Palmers get some sleep now, hear?' Buck cautioned as they left.

'As if we need to be told,' a relieved young girl laughed as the door swung closed. 'Who wouldn't want to sleep after an experience such as we've just had, papa?'

Colonel Palmer smiled, nodded, but didn't respond. Right at that moment, relieved and upbeat in the wake of a potential disaster, the colonel was about as far from sleep as a man could get. By his standards, this night was still quite young.

★ ★ ★

Donovan stared. Down below, he saw the unmistakable figure of the colonel somewhat furtively hurry down the gangplank to the jetty and hail the last horse cab in sight.

The gambler-gunman couldn't believe his luck. Acting on orders, he'd set up the big game in the salon with the express purpose of cleaning Palmer out. Smarter men than himself knew the colonel's habits, were aware he was not in a position to lose large sums — that an inveterate gambler like himself would feel compelled to rush off someplace and try to recoup. There was also the known fact that Palmer had a taste for the wilder side of life, and the dealer's boss had assured him that the lure of more gambling plus pretty young women would surely draw their quarry ashore after being cleaned out and in a way, humiliated.

Everything hinged on Palmer heading for the cat house after losing big.

But when Cole Vallantry horned in and reversed his fortunes, the dealer had figured he'd failed.

The sight of the cab rattling away in the direction of the wilder side of town brought a huge smile of relief to his sharp features and saw him heading smartly for the gangplank.

This night was far from over.

★　★　★

Buck Vallantry shivered in the night wind, realized he should have worn a jacket. Trouble was, since he'd come down the gangplank to stand on the exposed jetty with the midnight wind blowing unfettered across the river, and deep watery noises rising from below, it had become cold as a step-mother's kiss and was growing colder by the minute.

'Too close to the desert,' he muttered, then turned his back to the wind to shelter his hands while he built and lighted a Bull Durham.

He flicked the vesta away and looked up. A tall lean silhouette stood leaning against the ship's rail gazing out over the sleeping town.

Buck's scowl cut deep. His brother was part night-owl, he believed. He'd shown that out in the arid lands. He'd also demonstrated generosity on several occasions, yet none of that had been in evidence when the colonel's distraught daughter had arrived at their cabin some time ago to report her father had left the vessel. His brother had flatly refused to accompany Buck ashore to go look for the man.

'Enough is enough,' he'd protested. 'You know I'm up to my armpits on a big job of work for Headquarters, and I'm not going to get it done playing nursemaid to any randy old geezer who can't keep it in his pants and can't stay home nights.'

Buck considered that a pretty offensive way for a man to talk, especially with the daughter within earshot. Certainly it seemed both foolish and maybe a tad suspicious for Palmer to quit the Belle in the middle of the night, but he still didn't see the need for Cole to blacken the man's name by suggesting he'd maybe gone off tom-catting.

He'd objected but it fell on deaf ears.

'And what else would he be doing?' Cole had countered, and he'd found it hard to come up with a convincing response.

'OK, OK, get on with it, cowboy,' he chided himself, turning to go. 'Just go find the man and fetch him back yourself. Can't be that many places he could be in a town this size.'

The town called Placerville in which Buck Vallantry found himself on that bright, icy night proved much larger than he'd figured: a sturdy, scattered blend of the West's old and new set well back from the river, which was the town's life blood.

Over the next half hour he discovered that the town was virtually two, named unimaginatively Old Town and New.

Old Town had been old before the war and over recent years had deteriorated into a seedy slum that at times attracted some of the seediest characters in the southern sector of the territory. To Old Town gravitated the broke, the bad, the unlucky and the lost, with occasionally an influx of genuine hardcases and outlaws who could test the law's resources to the limit.

Old Town was thin gruel, cigarette butts and cardboard in the shoes to keep out the mud, while New Town, closer to the river, was French-fried steak, twenty-cent cigars and forty-dollar boots.

He paused on a corner to glance back at New Town. It was like a respectable morgue at this late hour. Ahead, Old Town at first appeared to be nothing but darkened dwellings, battered livery stables, a soup kitchen with a flapping tin roof, unpaved streets and battered sidewalks.

And the faintest strains of music.

Pricking his ears, he stared westward

along the curve of the street and caught a faint glow of light glancing off a rooftop. Without much enthusiasm he headed off to investigate, shoulders hunched, hands deep in the pockets and thinking about the hills.

Satchequaw Hills embraced most of the high mesa country to the south, which he visited once or twice a year to replenish his equine stock. Down there the air was clear and a man didn't meet up with any slinky gamblers or Stan Dover men, just mainly beautiful country, pretty weather and mustangs.

In his mind's eye he pictured the wild horses streaming across an upland meadow, heads high, uncut manes and tails flowing, running, running like greased joy and daring one solitary man with just two catch horses and a bunch of ropes to challenge them and their freedom, if he had the stones for it.

His little horse ranch up north was proof that he was more often successful than not. He still had hopes of getting down there during this visit, even though there was now an unexpected obstacle looming. He no longer could picture Cole showing ready to rough it in the mesa country and spending his days trying to rope wild horses who'd gladly tromp him to sawdust, as he'd seemed to be some days earlier.

But who could be sure? Maybe Cole would prove more accommodating than he showed? Maybe, behind that tough dude surface, he was just as delighted by their reunion as he was. And what better way to celebrate and cement their good fortune than by working together, making money and really getting to know each other all over again?

Minutes later found him staring across Ringo Street at the unexpected — a squat, solid-looking, two-story building with light and sound spilling from the ground floor, which appeared to be a bar room.

The music was coming from over there, and as he drew closer he saw the name above the door: Maisie's. Strange name for a saloon. Then the nickel dropped when he peered through a chink in a window curtain and glimpsed several full-figured women in glittering costumes, dancing, drinking or chatting with the customers.

The men didn't look like Old Town. Most of them appeared well-heeled and flashily dressed. New Town players, he decided. Players in the oldest game of all.

He sighed and frowned.

Might not Lauren Palmer be deeply offended if he was to go looking for her silver-headed old daddy in a cat-house in the middle of the night?

Next question: what option did he have? The rest of Placerville was dark, dead and laid to rest. Where else could a sprightly old dude like the colonel be this time of night?

He stepped back and stared upwards. The second floor, which he saw could be reached by an outside stairway rising from a side alley, was fully curtained off at every window, with narrow chinks of yellow light peering through here and there.

He shrugged. Nothing else for it but to go take a look inside, he supposed.

He was making his way toward the batwings when he spotted the badge-toter approaching along the plankwalk. He halted and massaged his jaw. At a glance this lawman looked the rugged capable kind, such a one who might well have heard something about the altercation aboard the Belle earlier. Then, realizing that the need for a little information outweighed all other considerations, he stepped out into the light and tipped hat brim respectfully.

'Evening, Sheriff. Or, guess a man could say, good morning, huh?'

The badgeman was heavily built with a bulldog jaw. He eyed the tall figure up and down, didn't seem either offended or impressed by what he saw.

'Do I know you, boy?'

'Just arrived in your fair town, Sheriff. Buck Vallantry is the name.'

'What's your business in Placerville?'

'Er, just passing through. Passenger on board the Dixie Belle as a matter of fact.' He put on a sober face. 'Might as well level with you, sir. A feller went drifting from off the Belle and folks are worried some.' He jerked his chin at the lighted building. 'Thought I'd take a look inside, seeing as though it's about the only place open.'

'I've heard all the excuses for coming to places like this,' came the sour response. 'Why don't you fellers just admit you can't leave it alone and let it go at that?'

He was about to turn away when a thought struck him. He paused. 'Sheriff, you ever hear of a man named Singleman down here this way?'

The man stiffened. 'Singleman?' He leaned closer, hard eyes narrowed. 'What's that name to you, boy? Do you know him by any chance?'

'Heck no. Just met a feller who happened to let slip that he might be interested in, er, talking to this man.

Sounds like he's no stranger to you, Sheriff?'

The man turned his head and spat, suddenly looking older and very tired.

'Seems everyone knows that name but nobody knows the *hombre* what goes by it,' he said bitterly. He shrugged. 'Yeah, I've heard of him, I even got paper on him at the office. Slick, crafty, brainy and way too smart to get caught for anything he's done or is supposed to have done, that's Singleman, or at least how I figure him. He was a big wheel up north and folks say he might be again. Politics, you know. It's wide open up there, so I hear tell, and that *hombre* all but ran Steuben County once, so I believe. But for mine he might as well be a ghost or a phantom. Every dang crime that goes unsolved, they start in claiming it must have been him. Kidnap, murder, grand larceny or stealing cookies off your ma. It's easier to lay all that stuff at the feet of a man that mightn't even exist than go off looking for the real crooks . . . '

The man's voice trailed away. Suddenly he looked haggard and spent, as though just mention of that name was a heavy burden. Muttering, he turned for the doors and shouldered his way inside, leaving Vallantry scratching his neck.

So much for trying to give Cole a hand in his manhunt, he mused.

He followed the sheriff of Placerville through the swinging doors and sauntered across to the long mahogany bar to order beer.

No sign of a ramrod erect figure in a planter's white suit and with a roguish eye.

By the time he'd been there an hour he felt he'd asked about the colonel of just about everybody, including the vast and brassy lady he supposed to be Maisie. She'd made a 'joke' of his query.

'You are looking for an old gray man, honeychile?' she'd shrieked like one of Macbeth's witches, giving him a nudge that nearly knocked him off his feet. 'I can do a lot better than that for you, boyo. I got me a whole mess of perky little gals here. C'mon and I'll introduce you to one.'

He passed up the offer and checked out the two tough looking characters minding the staircase. It didn't take long to realize that if you didn't go upstairs with a girl you just didn't get upstairs: rules of the house.

He decided he was going up anyway and headed for the exit.

He almost got away with it. He spotted another hardcase posted on the outside stairs, but gave the man the slip by shinning up a drainpipe to reach the upper level. Shucking his boots, he moved soundlessly along the gallery to peer into a lighted window here, paused to listen at another there.

No sight or sound of the hero of Telamachut Falls.

He was on the verge of giving it best when he glimpsed a light flicker on back along the gallery. He retraced his steps and identified Maisie's tones while still ten feet from the half-open window.

'Look, your client didn't pay, Lucille. Two hours up here with you, and not one white dime. And I didn't even see him leave, nor did the boys. Just how'd he manage that?'

'M-Maisie,' replied a quavering young voice. 'Just after the colonel left, I think I heard something — just before that old feller disappeared.'

'Like what?'

'Well, like a scuffle, I guess. And then just after that I heard someone on the back stairs.'

'Nobody ever uses the back stairs but me. Besides, I've got the only key.'

'I . . . I reckon I heard a key turning in a lock too, Maisie . . .'

Buck Vallantry didn't hear any more. A floorboard creaked and he whirled to see the staircase guard rushing him on stealthy feet. The man charged. Buck drew back his right fist, ducked low then hammered a punch right to the point of the jaw.

The man crashed unconscious to the floor and Buck stepped over him and was down the stairs in a flash. Reaching ground level he bolted into the dark, legged it down an alley then crossed several vacant blocks to reach New Town finally, blowing like a spent horse.

He was heading for the jailhouse to inform the sheriff what he'd overheard when he belatedly realized that lights were being lit and the street was beginning to come alive as citizens emerged, waving their arms and talking excitedly.

What in hell was going on?

A kid came running towards him, yelling excitedly. Buck seized him by the arm and held onto him.

'What is it, kid? he demanded. 'What's all the fuss?'

'Ain't you heard, mister? Someone's gone missin'. Some rich feller and — '

'Who?' he barked, feeling a chill. 'Who was it?'

'Er, some joker called the colonel, mister.'

The kid pulled loose and Buck glanced around to see Cole running towards him down the street.

4

A Bullet Says Goodbye

'Your goddamned colonel, again,' Cole Vallantry panted irritably. 'First he gets cleaned out by a sharp who couldn't fleece Granny Arbuckle, then he slips out on his daughter in the middle of the night like a kid playing hooky. Now she's hauled me out of bed to go look for both you and him.' He paused, gesturing irritably at the milling citizens. 'What are they stirred up about?'

'Same thing you're griping about, I guess. The word's out that the colonel's gone missing. From what I saw and heard at the cat house, it could be right.'

'You were at Maisie's? I thought you were the clean-cut country boy — '

'I was looking for her father, damnit! Didn't Lauren tell you?' Buck turned at a query from an old man wearing an overcoat over his nightshirt. 'No . . . I don't know where the colonel is, pops . . . ' His brow puckered. 'But how come everyone's up out of bed claiming he's gone missing of a sudden anyhow? Who says so?'

The oldtimer gestured dumbly in the direction of the jailhouse. As the brothers strode toward the squat stone building with the barred windows and a tin star nailed to a porch support, Cole Vallantry peered about in puzzlement.

'I just don't get it. You'd think it was the governor or someone gone missing. Why all the fuss?'

'The colonel's a war hero down here, man. All over this part of the territory and up north for that matter.'

'Are you talking about that backyard dust-up they call the battle of Telamachut Falls?' Buck nodded his head tersely and the other went on. 'That was no great victory. It was no more than a skirmish.'

'Not to them it wasn't.' Buck paused a beat, then added, 'Nor to me.'

Cole propped on a dime, searching his face. 'What are you saying . . . ?' His jaw dropped. 'You were South?'

'Right. So, what were you?'

It seemed a long silent moment passed before Cole Vallantry found his voice. 'I rode with the North.'

It was a significant moment. Both realized it. They'd discussed many things since their reunion including the War Between The States, but somehow the matter of alliance or allegiances hadn't arisen.

Yet neither man chose to comment as they continued on, though the moment of revelation had reminded both of just how much time and history had flown by during their long years apart.

They were weary-legged and testy by the time they agreed to stop by back at the docks to see if maybe the wanderer had returned. The jetty was ablaze with lights with people coming and going. They had no trouble picking out Lauren standing on the lower deck amongst a group of fellow passengers.

Cole led the way up the gangplank and the girl greeted them eagerly.

'You've found him?' she began, then cut off, seeing their faces. 'Oh my Lord, you were my last hope.' She clasped a hand over her heart. 'Now I know something terrible's happened to Father. He's always been a wanderer and a night-owl, but I never thought he'd be foolish enough to go ashore in a strange town at his age and at this time of night . . . '

The Vallantrys traded glances. Both knew some old boys like the colonel. They were prey to the old wants and urges, and seldom took kindly to good advice or caution when they felt like kicking over the traces.

'There's a lot of buffalo dust being talked all over,' Cole reassured, gesturing at the people on the jetty. 'Buck and I reckon he might have just had a couple too many and might have found a quiet place to sleep it off.'

'That crabby old sheriff said Father may have been involved in some kind of disturbance at some awful place called Maisie's,' Lauren retorted, looking from one to the other.

Buck glanced at the stars and Cole checked out the time on his pocket watch. The girl nodded as though accepting their silence as affirmation of what she'd been told. For a moment she seemed about to cry, but then instead started in talking, telling them of their plans for the colonel to retire at last from his active life in both political power-broking and his ongoing role as commander of the Free Citizens Militia of Steuben County where it still existed as some sort of quasi-official regulatory outfit with powers and status not that far removed from those of a regular army unit.

It was interesting new information that painted a broader picture of the colonel for Cole Vallantry. But Buck visited Steuben County from time to time in his travels and had been aware of the missing man's status from the outset.

Lauren was recounting a recent amusing incident involving her father and the governor when a kid clutching a brown paper envelope forced his way up the gangplank, calling Lauren's name.

'Over here, kid!' Buck hollered, and passengers gave way as the tousle-haired ten-year-old threaded through them.

'Message for you, Miss Palmer,' he panted, all freckles and curly red mop beneath the tattered wreck of a seaman's cap.

'Thanks, kid,' said Cole, flipping him a quarter.

'Thank you, mister.' The kid grinned and vanished back into the crowd as Lauren tore the envelope open with trembling fingers. She scanned the contents and her face turned the color of old chalk.

'No!' she gasped, the slip of paper tumbling from her fingers. 'No . . . '

The Vallantrys traded stares before Cole bobbed down and retrieved the note.

'What's it say?' Buck demanded.

87

'Listen. 'Miss Palmer, your father is in our hands. He won't be hurt unless you or anybody else tries to find him, in which case we'll send you his head in a sack. Be warned. We play for keeps.''

Cole looked up. 'No signature.'

Buck started in cussing. Then he remembered there was a lady present. Then, belatedly, he remembered something else.

'That kid!' he hissed, and started off.

'By Judas, he's right,' Cole said urgently. He seized the girl by the wrists. 'Lauren, just wait here with the Belle. Wait and have confidence in us. If we can find that kid we might find out who gave him the note. And don't worry. We'll find the colonel.'

He didn't wait for a reply. His flying feet took him through the press of people and down the gangway, then across the crowded jetty with no beg-pardons. Leaping high, he glimpsed Buck's figure already out in the street and raced after him.

By the time he'd reached the street,

Buck was nowhere to be seen. He cursed. Glancing right and left he sighted the street that passed through the central block, took off in that direction. Fast-stepping past staring citizens, he covered a half-block before suddenly spotting his brother across the street beneath an awning. He was talking to the messenger boy.

By the time he got across the street Buck was handing the kid a dollar.

'OK, son, much obliged,' he drawled, then turned to nod to Cole. 'He doesn't know the joker who gave him the note, but he sure gives a good description. Here, kid, tell my brother what this joker looked like.'

The kid puffed out his chest, proud to be the sudden center of attention.

'Well, he was tall and kinda mean-lookin' and was wearin' a long gray duster and one of them hard-hitter hats. His eyes were kinda shiny black and scary and he had a skinny little mustache.'

'Seen him?' Buck queried.

Cole shook his head. 'No. But like you say, it's a good description.' He took out another coin and gave it to the boy. 'Well done, kid. You've been a big help, but I'd lie low and keep mum from here on in just in case he might still be about and doesn't take kindly to you talking. Savvy?'

The kid's eyes widened and he was off, vanishing down the nearby alley in a twinkle.

'Let's get looking — ' Buck began, but the other interrupted.

'I'll start the search. I'll cut back to the Belle and get the captain to delay sailing time.'

'But — '

'You want to get this manhunt under way or do you want us to stand here debating like a couple of damned politicians?'

Buck's scowl showed his resentment. Although the other was older and more experienced, he still felt he had more native savvy and know-how to draw on at a time like this. Did he want to show his brother he was boss? Maybe. But he couldn't argue with reality. Time was at a premium.

'Where are you starting?' he snapped, turning to go.

'Riverside.'

'Then I'll head for Old Town. We'll scour this burg end to end if we have to. Be careful.'

'You too.'

Cole Vallantry shook his head wonderingly as he watched Buck take off down the alley the kid had taken. Had he ever had anyone to warn him to take care? If he had, he'd forgotten. It felt good, or at least as good as anything could at such a time.

The scarred walls of Old Town were visible ahead when Buck emerged from the long and winding alleyway. He loosed the Colt in its holster then left his hand upon it as the dark and fang-roofed buildings closed about him like a shroud.

* * *

'Sorry, Mr Vallantry,' the captain said regretfully, 'but we're just about to get under way.'

'But damn it all man, there's been a kidnapping and there's not been enough time to follow through on it. We just can't leave — '

'Sorry.' The captain was firm now. 'I've already delayed departure an hour due to this misadventure, but my schedule won't tolerate any further tardiness.'

The portly figure turned to Lauren standing at the foot of the gangplank, the focus of attention for the still considerable crowd. 'You understand, I'm sure, Miss Palmer? Company schedules, y'know?'

Lauren had plainly recovered from her shock, displaying a strength that impressed everybody, including a hard-to-impress Cole Vallantry.

'Of course, Captain, and I appreciate your delaying sailing for this long.' She turned to Vallantry. 'Naturally I've had our luggage taken ashore, Cole. I'll book a room at the hotel and just wait.' She forced a smile and proffered a gloved hand. 'I'll never be able to thank you and Buck enough for your kindness.'

The hand went unclaimed. A scowling Cole Vallantry removed his low-crowned dark hat and swabbed perspiration from his forehead. His expression was unreadable but behind the taut mask of his handsome face he was fighting a battle of epic proportions: Cole Vallantry versus Cole Vallantry.

Every instinct told him to simply shake hands with the girl and cut adrift from his brother right now. He'd cooled down and was now looking squarely at reality. He'd set out from Colorado on a high-risk manhunt that, if successful, could set him up for life and save him for all time from the flashy, half-smart, half-successful existence that his wits, guns and self-confidence had enabled him to live ever since quitting the Arkansas back-hills seemingly half a lifetime ago.

He'd become an expert on Single-man through an amalgam of vague clues, whispers, hunches and the odd fragment of genuine information that had led him to believe his quarry was located someplace down here along the Rogue.

There'd been no sign of his man in Placerville. But Rivertown was a city compared to this burg, a big place with big men and big money where a big-time shaker and mover like Single-man might feel most at home.

So, he would sail west with the Belle and Buck could make up his own mind whether to follow or linger here and play hero.

He swung to face the girl with iron in his face — met again the impact of those wonderful eyes — then heard his own strange voice say treacherously, 'Captain, have your hands get our gear off and off-load the horses. We're staying on.'

He vaguely remembered Lauren throwing her arms about his neck. He was trying not to remember other moments in time when the characteristically cool and clear-thinking Cole Vallantry demonstrated he could act like a damn fool just as well as anybody.

* * *

Buck Vallantry knelt on one knee on a grassy bank beside the river, cupped his hands into the water and drank. When he came erect he found his brother ruefully surveying the empty whiskey flask in his hand.

'Plenty of good water,' he grunted, sleeving his mouth.

'Plenty everything. Water, slums, bullet-headed lawmen, brain-dead towners, darkness, cold and sore feet. Plenty everything except leads. We might as well face it, cowboy, we're beat and this task is plainly beyond us. We should have taken the Belle when we had the chance after all, for all the good we've been here.'

Buck just grinned toughly and

started to walk away. He'd learned his brother liked to dramatize on occasion. It was Cole who'd ordered their stuff off the Belle, he who'd set the pace over the past two frustrating and exhausting hours. When he looked over his shoulder his brother was following; slow, but following.

Soon they were back in the wagon-rutted main stem. Scarce anybody about now.

★   ★   ★

It was time for Buck Vallantry to ride back to town. In the hour before first light the countryside was black as the inside of a cow and had been ever since he'd set out, in truth. He realized now it had simply been frustration that had driven him to saddle up and begin circling the outskirts of town in the hope of maybe picking up the trail of the kidnappers, whom he was by now dead certain had quit Placerville with the colonel.

He'd found nothing, had only succeeded in wearying both himself and his horse. Yet he knew, as sure as he knew anything, he would be back out here amongst the tall trees and rolling hillsides just as soon as the sun came up.

He and Cole, he hoped.

Dim lights from the main street reached out for him as the heavy footed horse carried him in a time later. The town was silent, asleep, exhausted by all the excitement. The only place showing lights through open doors at this ungodly hour was the jailhouse, where he found Cole spooning sorghum into a mug of black coffee while the sheriff sat behind his spur-scarred desk laboriously writing out his report.

A dab hand at the bookwork was the sheriff of the river town but less impressive at dealing with major crime.

At least that was Cole's evaluation of the man as he joined Buck on the warped-board front porch and waited for first light.

Buck just grunted. His thoughts were still out along the trail where he'd had the opportunity to do some reckoning in the mopoke-haunted dark.

'The Flintlocks are my best bet,' he grunted.

'Huh?'

He gestured westward. 'The Flintlock Hills lie some twenty miles southwest. Mean country slashed by canyons half a mile deep and hills so steep even the wild horses keep away.' He nodded. 'Uh huh, if I'd kidnapped someone and was looking for a fine place to hole up and hide out while I claimed the ransom, then the Flintlocks would be my first pick.'

Cole stared at him. 'You believe they'll claim a ransom?'

'What else?'

Cole shook his head. 'Never occurred to me. I guess that after listening to you bore me half to death telling me what a national hero and king of the pony soldiers he is up in Utah, that Palmer's disappearance would have something to do with power and politics, not just dirty money.'

Buck blinked slowly.

'You know, I hadn't thought of that. But maybe you could be right and — '

He broke off, diverted by the small figure emerging from the gloom of the street at the run. He blinked and got to his feet with a frown. 'It's the messenger kid.' He raised his voice. 'Hey! What are you doing still up at this hour?'

'Mister! I just seen him!'

'The colonel?' Cole said, jumping up.

The panting boy shook his head. 'No, mister, the feller what gave me the message.'

Buck was first to reach the boy, hunkering down before him.

'Are you sure, sonny?'

'Certain sure,' came the quick reply. Turning, the boy pointed to the mouth of Abbey Street a short distance south. 'There's an old warehouse down yonder we play outlaws sometimes. I was snooping around like I've been all night, you know, looking for that man they took away . . . hopin' to make some more money if I found him, I guess. Well, I got tired a spell back and sat down in the dark across the street from the warehouse. I guess I was nodding off when I thought I heard something. I looked up, and there he was up on the half-landing by the old winch, looking up and down the street like he was real scared. Or maybe it was his leg . . . '

'You dead certain it was the same man, kid?' Cole pressed.

'Sure was, mean-lookin' thin feller in flashy-looking coat and hat with them beady eyes. Only now he's got a limp.'

The brothers traded looks.

'He seems sure,' said Buck. He shook his head. 'But that doesn't make any kind of sense. There ain't a town between here and Washington where you won't stretch rope for kidnap. Why would you hang around?'

Cole answered his question with another, for the boy: 'How could you know he was limping if he was up in the loft?'

'It was when he turned to go back inside. I could see him holding the railing with one hand and kinda lifting the bad leg with the other. Could be I even heard him grunting.'

'Are you saying those hellions might still be right here in town?'

The voice came from the doorway. The sheriff was standing there, white-faced and pop-eyed. The man was trembling.

'Don't give yourself an attack, man,' Buck said disgustedly, rising. His Colt .45 suddenly filled his fist as he turned to Cole. 'We'll take care of this.'

'And right now,' Cole affirmed.

The kid coughed. They stared at him a moment before understanding.

Both fished for cash and left him pop-eyed and grinning as they jumped off the porch and jogged toward Abbey Street.

The upper sections of the warehouse were lost in the thick darkness. A sheet of newspaper rustled down the fetid street before a pre-dawn zephyr. Gun hammers clicked as they stood beneath a stunted cottonwood staring up. There was nothing to be seen so there was nothing else to be done than what they did.

Cole led the way across to the wagon entrance and the blackness of the structure engulfed them. Moving across the earthen floor, each was barely able to distinguish the silhouette of the other as they approached the sagging, broken staircase. Ears straining, guns at the cock, they waited, listening. The night blackness was thick with silence.

Buck had mastered the art of total silence and immobility waiting in blinds for wild mustangs to trap themselves in his rope binds, sometimes for what seemed forever. He was impressed to note after several minutes that a statue-like Cole was at least his match in that area. And thought proudly: 'We do make a good team.'

A board creaked somewhere above,

then all was still again.

But it was enough.

'Someone up there right enough,' Buck barely breathed. The gun glinted in his fist and his dim face was as taut and hard as pressed steel in the thick blackness. 'Gotta take him alive, bro. Gotta find out off of him where the colonel's been taken.'

Cole nodded curtly and they began to climb together. Stealth was not a possibility. Ancient risers creaked and groaned like sinners in torment beneath their boots and soon chunks of rotted timbers were breaking off and thudding to the dirt below as they now ascended fast.

'Give yourself up! We've got the place surrounded!'

Cole's sudden shout brought a flock of little bats bursting out of their hideaways above to go flapping out through the hay loft into the night. Beneath the racket, both men clearly heard it . . . step, drag . . . step, drag . . .

As they gained the landing, Buck shoved his gun high and touched off a shot that hammered the eardrums.

'Freeze up, kidnapper!' he shouted. He fired again and the echoes were slow to fade, replaced by total silence. There could be only one explanation. The man must have gone to ground again. Waiting for them.

But as yet there was no answer to the other question: was he alone?

That thought preoccupied both as they began climbing a second rickety stair. With just three steps before reaching the top level, Buck called out.

'We know you gave the message to the kid, pilgrim, so we know you're tied up in the kidnapping. Last chance to give yourself up and do a deal!'

No response.

Impatiently, Cole thrust ahead and used the muzzle of his gun to push open the half door. It creaked open and they realized the first light had come since they'd entered the building. An old desk, a broken chair, a dim door that moved . . .

'Down!' Buck roared and both dropped flat as the head-splitting reverberation of a .45 going off in a confined space engulfed them.

They returned fire together, leaping tongues of yellow gun flame casting hellish light over fetid walls, the crash and insanity of excessive gunfire.

The old door fell off under the fusillade and they were concentrating fire on the dim gray room beyond it when an unseen gun bellowed and a slug kissed Cole's right shoulder.

Two heads jerked up as one. There was a split second to take in the reality of a sprawled figure supported on uncovered roof-beams triggering down at them. The slugs hammered through planking, crossbeams and stair risers. But not living flesh. The gunman knew where they were but couldn't actually see them.

Upon that realization they opened up together, coughing on gunsmoke, deafened by the racket. But there was visibility to see the smoking Colt tumble down first, followed moments later by the gunman himself who struck the rickety floor hard on his back and stayed there.

After what seemed a long time, Cole reached out a long right arm and touched the muzzle to the motionless man's temple.

'Any more of you here?' he hissed.

Feebly, the man shook his head.

'Just me . . . ' The voice sounded vaguely familiar. 'Just me . . . dumped and left to fend for myself . . . ' A catch in the throat. 'No respect . . . but who respects a gambling man . . . not Hatch, that's for sure . . . '

The brothers traded glances. The floor was soaked with blood and it was plain to a blind man that the pistoleer was dying. Together they rose up out of the ladder well and the moment they saw his face plainly, recognition hit. It was Donovan the crooked dealer from the Dixie Belle!

They dropped on their knees by his side, both barking questions. But

Donovan was already beyond hearing. It was amazing the dealer could still talk with all that lead inside him as he filtered in and out of consciousness, bitterness keeping him alive.

' . . . I was good enough for the job of fleecing the colonel on the Belle so's he'd have to go running off to the whorehouse to try and win his stake back . . . '

The voice cut off. They thought he was gone. Cole shook his shoulder. The slow eyelids opened to stare at the last sunrise hue.

'We snatched him good and got him away . . . and I was as good as off with them before that mongrel hoss kicked my leg and busted it . . . then all I was good for was staying behind and delivering the note while they . . . while they . . . '

An ugly throat sound. Buck shook the man's shoulder again. The head lolled to one side.

'Is he dead, Cole?'

'He's not alive.'

5

Searching for Sign

Along the passageway leading into the cells, a caged drunk wrangled in his sleep with all his enemies, the faithless women, lawmen who didn't understand him, slick dudes who cheated at cards and the worst enemies of all, those people who tried to save him.

The sheriff shifted a cud of chewing tobacco from one side of his mouth to the other, the chair creaking beneath his weight.

'Git that door, deppity.'

The deputy closed off the passage-way door and it was quiet in the office again. The sheriff's eyelids were drooping. He'd been up all night and didn't figure he would get any sleep today.

'Well, I guess we're done here,' Buck

Vallantry said, setting his hat on his head.

'Done?' the sheriff said dully. 'Wish I was done. OK for you fellers. You blow a man out of his boots and then blow town, leaving me to handle all the paper work and the questions ... and of course the visit from the high-and-mighty marshal's office.

As if wearied by the simple effort of speaking, the man leaned back against his chair and waved a mottled hand.

'But off you go. Don't you worry none about me or what I have to d — '

'Damned right we won't worry!' Cole had suddenly heard enough gripe. 'You had a man kidnapped under your big nose, you had a gang of outlaws in your town and didn't even know it, and you were no help at all when we got the tip on Donovan and went after the son of a bitch.' He slammed the flat of his hand down hard on the desktop, causing the by now wide-eyed lawman to jump. 'You're not a sheriff's bootlace!'

'I guess that goes for me too,' Buck

said. He didn't sound sure. He'd had little experience in bucking peace-officers, but his brother seemed to be expert at it. He nodded. 'You sure you don't have anything on Donovan in your files, Sheriff?'

'Not a purblind thing,' the sheriff replied, getting up and slapping an opened file on the desk with the back of his hand. 'Been through it end to end — nothing.' He squinted at them, his manner subservient now. 'You sure you fellers — I guess I should call you heroes — ain't overlooked anything I could use in the investigation?'

Cole scowled and shook his head. He moved to the window and stared out. Placerville appeared to be in a state of shock. Across the street, he glimpsed Lauren Palmer seated on the gallery of the fancy women's-wear store. She wasn't weeping anymore.

He turned back and looked quizzically at his brother. Buck had already announced his intention of hunting down the colonel and his kidnappers.

Trailing was the thing he did best next to horse-breaking. Cole hadn't said he wouldn't be joining him, but he hadn't said he would be either. Buck supposed he couldn't blame him, although he would still like to talk him round if he could. He focused on what his brother was saying:

'This has all the hallmarks of a professional job, Sheriff. The timing, the way they went about it, the fact that Palmer is an important figure up north.' Cole shook his head. 'No sir, no hick operation this. Which means your town was staked out by some genuine heavyweights, and they weren't invisible. You must have noticed strange faces over the past few days. Someone who looked like big-time trouble. Hard men flashing their money around or making a splash. Come on, think, man, think.'

'No-good two-timin' bitch!' came a shriek from the cells, then silence again.

'That Harry Coogan,' the lawman said with a half grin, then sobered when he looked at two hard faces. He rubbed his forehead and his wandering eye fell on his opened files ledger before him. He frowned at something he saw, then put his finger on a question mark in pencil alongside a name. He brightened. He wanted to give the Vallantrys something, anything that might get them out of his place and leave him be.

'Well, there was this story a drunk blabbed out to me a couple of days back. He was a stranger from downriver who fancied himself some kind of tough guy until I threw him in the slammer then kicked his sorry ass out of town next morning . . . '

The sheriff paused and puffed out his chest in recollection of his moment.

'Get on with it,' Cole growled.

'Oh yeah. Well, this bum reckons he was settin' out front of the Double Dice late this night, nobody around but him all alone there in the dark, when this big flash coach and four comes gliding down Main, you know, almost like a ghost outfit or something in the moonlight. But it was real enough and the bum is watching it go by on big rubber-tired wheels when this joker leans from the window to ash a big cigar and he gets a real good look at him.'

He paused for effect.

'He swears he'd seen this feller downriver once a year ago. Guy name of Singleman.'

Suddenly Cole Vallantry wasn't in any hurry to go anyplace. Drawing out a chair with the toe of his boot, he produced his cigars and offered the case to a startled lawman. This could be a long session.

* * *

It was just a murmur at first, a faint whisper of sound in the stillness of the early morning not caused by wind or gopher, skirling birds or a coming change of the weather.

It rose, it fell and then became clearer, a steady relentless drumbeat

drawing ever closer over the gentle high
country swells until it became identifi-
able as the hammer of iron-hard
unshod hoofs coming hard across the
uplands.

Abruptly the stallion rushed into full
view, running as only an animal that
had never known confining fence, rope
or boundary could, seeming to flow
over the coarse yellow grass as though
fashioned from something lighter than
hide, hoof and bone.

It was an ugly runt.

Nothing of the sleek thoroughbred
stallion with its pampered air of
aristocracy remained about this one.
That had been ground out of the breed
over the years and the decades. It was a
savage creature of the wilds, its hard
hide scarred by fang and claw with a
redness in the eye and bottle-nosed
head held high with pride in not what it
was not, but what it was.

The stallion halted in mid-stride with
dust wisping away from sturdy, tireless
legs. It stood listening and soon heard

them coming after him. He tossed his head and stamped a foot in impatience, for he was an aristocrat and they are by nature intolerant and impatient of lesser ones than themselves.

Moments later the hill behind was covered with them, the surging wild herd, all undersized, lean and unkempt but covering the land with that same matchless ease until they resembled an avalanche of life bearing down upon the leader of the pack.

The stallion emitted a piercing shriek and was off again in one great bound, showing them the way down to the bottom lands, reminding them by his virile example of what they were and would always be, free and unconquerable.

As suddenly as they'd come they were gone with only the slow subsiding dust to mark their passing.

The watcher strained to see them but something was wrong. The hillscape was breaking up in his vision and he was shaking. A hand grabbed his shoulder. He tried to shrug it off but now the voice intruded.

'I thought you were an early riser? C'mon, we've got outlaws to catch.'

The last dregs of the vivid dream faded as he sat up and stared dully at his brother. He cussed. That was his favorite dream. Cole grabbed a shirt off the bureau and tossed it at him and quit the room.

'Sure . . . outlaws,' Buck Vallantry muttered. And felt guilty, when only for a moment, he wished it was outlaw horses, not men, they would be searching for today.

★   ★   ★

The days were growing colder. The Vallantrys had spent the first night of their sweep of the river valley uplands in a sheepherder's abandoned shack where the night wind whistled through the uncaulked chinks, and where Buck had wanted to bring their mounts indoors out of the cold but Cole had vetoed the notion.

The second night they camped in the bottom of an unnamed creek after having combed miles of wagon trail, horse track and even animal pads across a wide area of some twenty square miles.

Howling wolves had kept them awake that night, a reminder of how close the wilderness really was to bustling big towns like Placerville.

Breakfast of beans, coffee and stale bread, then back in the saddle with still no sign of what they were searching for.

'Could be that dumb sheriff was right,' Cole growled an hour later as the sun came up to shed feeble light over the cold landscape. 'Could be, that with any job as well-planned and professional as that was, and maybe Singleman behind it, they spirited the colonel away on the river by boat?'

Buck shook his head as he leaned from the leather to stare at the bare earth of the single-horse track they were following.

'They're fishing up and down the

Rogue day and night back there. So a man with half a brain wouldn't risk the river. I doubt they'd even risk crossing it.' He straightened and made a sweeping gesture. 'Southwest of the Rogue, they crossed it somewhere down here and all we've gotta do is find it. Bet on it.'

Cole stared at his brother sourly. 'Must be a good feeling to be right about everything every goddam day of your life?'

Buck's smile was easy. He could ride broken-gaited horses and sleep under the stars winter or summer and never feel it, or let it roughen his temper.

'Cheer up, man. This is only the beginning. If your badman is the nonesuch wonder desperado you paint him, and if your bosses in Colorado want him so mortal bad, then you should be the one geeing me up and lifting my spirits.'

'You know, if you'd have ever gone to college, you could have majored in jawbone. Why don't you — ?'

'Take a look down in yonder draw just in case they cut through there to avoid drawing too close to that way-station up ahead?' Buck interrupted amiably. 'Good notion, bro. Just follow me.'

Buck's half-wild Indian horse responded to a light pressure of the knees and it didn't improve Cole's early morning disposition to note that horse and rider both appeared lean, clean and log-jammed with energy and a keenness for the hunt as they loped away downslope, scaring the wood's birds out of the trees.

He was far from feeling that good despite the fact that he was still elated by the manner in which the name of Singleman had slipped out almost by accident back in Placerville, his first vague hint of contact with the man he hunted after long weeks on one long trail after another.

When Headquarters put the fat Singleman down before him, he'd thought, this will be a cinch. Stands to reason that anybody who'd been this prominent and well-recorded over a period of time couldn't simply disappear. He hadn't been manhunting a week before realizing that disappearing seemed exactly what the one-time political heavyweight and wanted criminal — at least in Colorado — had done.

He knew what he looked like, what his habits were, even who he'd helped in power up in Steuben County and those he'd brought down, had removed, possibly even 'disappeared.' But not one lead on where the man had vanished to or even if he was still alive.

Now he was all fired up again by what some insomniac drunk had seen at two o'clock on a dark night — or imagined he had done.

What he needed was a cigar.

He lighted up, drew deep and shook out his horse's bridle. The animal moved into a lope and he leaned back in the leather, trailing fragrant smoke. That was better. He set the Cuban between his teeth, then frowned. What was the cowboy doing now? Looked like he was waving him down into the arroyo with some impatience. What now?

He found out soon enough.

Wordlessly Buck indicated the arroyo floor which had plainly been recently built up by hand with rocks, deadfalls and debris to form a bed wide and strong enough to support a wagon above the mud. It was plain to the naked eye that it had seen recent use, with tracks of vehicles and horses leading up the low walls on either side.

They spent an hour combing the immediate area, backtracking the spoor of a rubber-wheeled heavy wagon and four or five outriders until it was lost on stony ground. To their northeast they found the spot where the cavalcade had quit the main Placerville-Wigfall trail. They followed the sign due west of the arroyo crossing for two hours until it linked up with the made road from the Arizona border, which Buck believed led all the way to Rivertown.

'Looks like the sheriff's bum was right, the sheriff was right and even we were right, Cole,' Buck said with grim triumph. He cocked an eyebrow as he twisted tobacco and rice paper into a neat white cylinder. 'Could be you were right about this Singleman too, huh?'

'That has to be too early to tell,' Cole insisted, jumping down to walk up and down the tracks. Then he paused to smile. 'But it has to be a chance.'

'It'd be some long coincidence if it did turn out that the guy you came hunting in the first place should turn out to be behind the colonel's kidnapping, don't you reckon?'

Cole turned sober as he folded his arms and talked straight.

'A coincidence? Sure. But maybe not such a big one. You see, bro, Singleman never touches anything small. If it's petty theft, a backshooting in an alley, even a bank swindle in the back blocks — forget it. But if it's the buying of judges, the manipulation of funds to affect the territory's balance of payments with Washington adversely, or some white-money-fuelled Indian insurrection in the gold mining country that leads to mine ownerships changing hands under suspicious circumstances — then you might look to see if Singleman's fine hand hasn't been involved.'

'Uh huh.' Buck Vallantry had little knowledge of such matters but was impressed by his kinsman's seeming knowledge of the world of the big-time criminal. 'So, you don't reckon kidnapping would be a bit of a come-down for a rare uppity bird like Singleman, then?'

'Everyday grabbing someone for ransom might be.' Cole nodded. 'Uh huh, if this is a Singleman crime, then it means one of two things. Either he's slipping from where he used to be, or else he's planning more use for Palmer than earning some ready cash by squeezing family and friends. If I had to guess, I'd have to say it's political. Singleman partially ran Steuben County once, and I don't have to remind you the colonel was some kind of hero figure up there.'

Buck stepped down and stretched. Feeble sunlight was slanting its way though gaunt branches. His cigarette was about smoked through. He took a last drag and flipped the butt away, watching Cole from the corner of his eye.

'What?' Cole said.

He shrugged.

'You don't say much about your job, do you?'

'What's to say? If the regular peace-officers can't find or catch some gang or outlaw they contact the Bureau of Criminal Justice in Denver. They examine the case and if they determine it warrants special attention they in turn contact the folks I work for. D.O.S.S.'

'D.O.S.S.?'

'Department Of Special Services. The department has men like me on its books — manhunters if you want to call us that. We're not tied to any city or county, just go after whoever they want brought in, wherever the hell they might be. Anything else you're curious about?'

'Guess not.'

'OK, then let's get on with it.' Cole indicated the fading tracks leading up over the western lip of the arroyo. 'You know this country some. What lies west from here?'

'Rough country as far as I know, then rangeland for about twenty miles leading down to Tumbleweed Valley and Rivertown.'

'Could just be Singleman country.'

'Mebbe.'

'What do you mean — mebbe?'

Buck shrugged.

'If you'll recall, the sheriff only said he thinks there's a joker of that name and he thinks he might come from this region, which covers a mighty big piece of ground.'

'Take it from me, brother, Singleman exists right enough. And he was seen at

Placerville right at the time of the kidnapping.'

'Seen by a drunk in the middle of a dark night.'

Cole Vallantry stared at his brother in silence for a long moment, frowning. Then he shrugged and said, 'What's the quickest way to make Rivertown? Cross-country or by the river?'

'By paddle-wheeler, of course.' Buck paused then added reluctantly, 'There's one leaving down-river at six tonight.'

'Then we'll be on it.'

'If you say so.'

'I say so, mister. Let's ride.'

6

The Exile

They covered ten miles along the Placerville road and got off to spell the horses at a bend where the wind was blowing hard through the big dark trees.

'OK,' Cole said, setting his cigar alight with a flashy pocket-flint, 'get it off your chest.'

Buck was easing his mount's saddle girth. 'Huh?'

'Let's talk straight, brother. We haven't been together long but I'm sure getting to know you. What are your reservations about what we're doing. It's crystal clear you've got some and I'd like to know what they are.'

Buck leaned an arm on his saddle and considered lying. He thought better of it, dropped his arm and moved off to stand upon a deadfall log from where he had a better view of the country ahead.

'The way I see it whoever snatched the colonel is mighty good at what they do and there seems to be a whole bunch of them. Seems to me that going after that kind of an outfit is a job for the law or even the army, not just a cowboy and . . . and whatever it is you are.'

Cole's stare hardened. 'Officially designated government manhunter is what I am. As for the odds, well I've bucked the odds all my life and I'm not about to quit now when that little lady is back in town crying her eyes out, and you and I are the only ones I've seen about who shape up as good enough and ready enough to do something about it. Goddamnit, man, the way you talked about the colonel I imagined you'd stick your hand in the flames for him. Explain.'

Buck looked at him levelly.

'OK, I will. Tell me, bro, would you

128

be as rip-snorting keen to thrash about the rough country like we've been doing for days, then be ready to jump on a boat and get down to Rivertown fast if the name of Singleman hadn't come up?'

Cole began pacing to and fro, plainly holding onto his temper.

'OK, so I'm hunting this big one and I mean to bag him. I won't deny it. But the chance that Singleman could be involved in this affair only doubles and trebles my determination to see this through. Howcome? The man's pure evil. If I listed all we know he's done and supposed to have done, you wouldn't sleep until we had that silver-headed war hero back safely with his daughter. Compassion first, nailing Singleman second. Savvy?'

Buck felt a faint twinge of guilt. Was he serious about the danger, or did he simply want to forget his sense of responsibility and go chase the mustangs through the tall and uncut? He was a horseman, not a manhunter. But surely any man could find excuses for not doing what he felt he should deep down.

'OK,' he sighed finally, returning to his horse. 'You've made your point, I guess.'

'No guessing, mister. The point is made. So, now we're agreed. We're going to see this thing through, right?'

'I said OK.'

'Not good enough. We're doing this and we're doing it my way. Keerect?'

That did it.

Buck turned so smoothly and unexpectedly from the horse that he seemed to reach his brother in the blink of an eye. A steel-stiff finger shot out and caught Cole in the chest with such force he was driven back three paces.

'If we do it at all we will do it our way, bucko,' he barked. 'Not yours or mine . . . ours! I'm ready to go just as far as you for the colonel, maybe even a step farther. And whether the *hombre* you're after is involved or not, I've seen and figured enough to know this might prove the most dangerous thing either of us have ever tried. But we're going to go about it as equal partners. You hear that word, hot-shot? Equal!'

Warring emotions chased one another across Cole Vallantry's face. At once he was mad, challenged, impressed. Mainly impressed. And in the end it was this that overrode his anger. Despite his brother's size and abilities, he realized he still regarded him as a kid. But the Buck Vallantry standing before him now, plainly ready to have it out with words, fists or even sixguns, was certainly no kid.

And that could only prove to his own selfish advantage in what lay ahead.

His charming grin flashed as he finally relaxed.

'Couldn't agree more, brother. Does a man good to get a thing off his chest, I always say. Clears the air. Ready to ride now?'

Buck didn't reply as he swung up and kicked away.

The journey to Placerville was made

mostly in silence. But by the time they'd finished putting their horses aboard the Betsy Anne, then visited the City Bathhouse for a relaxing one-hour soak in their huge oaken tubs, ruffled feathers were soothed and they were even able to joke some about their brush.

But things wouldn't be exactly the same as they had been. For Buck, the clash had only served to make him realize just how much he'd come to care for his long-lost brother, while at the same time sensing even more strongly than before that there might be a darker side to Cole, glimpses of which had shown throughout on the trail.

The change in Cole was less complicated. Although he'd realized from first meeting that the 'kid brother' was rugged and independent by nature, the day's events had revealed him as no sort of a kid at all but a man in the true sense of the word.

How that understanding might affect their association he didn't know. What he did know was that he now suspected he couldn't have a better ally and back-up if, in time, the colonel's disappearance did lead him to Singleman.

Like a gambler punting all on one last roll of the dice, Cole Vallantry had everything riding on his succeeding in what the authorities of several states and territories had failed to do over the years. Get Singleman.

* * *

Five in the morning on Rosedale Ranch. It was still dark with drifts of fog ghosting southwards from the river breaking silently against the high fences enclosing the sprawling headquarters of the remote highvalley ranch.

It was twenty miles to Rivertown but could have been a hundred due to the ranch's isolation. The nearest wagon trail lay five miles distant, the only vehicular route to Rosedale was the gravel trail leading in from the trail where a curious traveller would first encounter Keep Out signs and eventually sentries with rifles long before getting a glimpse of those high walls or see the sunlight glinting off the house's huge plate windows.

Little was known of Rosedale Ranch down along the river. Originally built and occupied by another recluse, it had lain empty and unwanted for years after he died until the current owner known only as Mr Brown took over with his armed retinue two years earlier.

If the original owner had been private and reclusive, Mr Brown — known in another life as Singleman — proved even more so — so much so that curiosity about the man and his minions eventually faded. Strange stories about Rosedale and its new owner circulated from time to time, and on several occasions some of the outfit's hardcase hands had been involved in shooting scrapes in the region. Why such events never seemed to lead to charges being laid was something of a mystery, although the word was that Mr Brown either intimidated the sheriff or otherwise influenced him not to take action.

At five-fifteen Singleman came down-stairs with a lightness of tread that belied his bulk. He was fully dressed at that hour as was his regular habit when in residence. He was met at the bottom of the massive redwood stairs by a man in livery who silently proffered a tray on which stood a steaming mug.

Singleman sipped his coffee as he proceeded through the great house, his boots making no sound upon the rich Brussels carpets.

Familiar sounds of activity reached him from other sections of the house. The day-to-day pattern at Rosedale Ranch when the master was in residence was strict. Early rising, working the blood-horses, maybe some shooting followed by breakfast in the Spanish Hall after which Singleman usually saw visitors. These could be all manner of men ranging from criminals and desperadoes up to men of power and influence in politics and industry, mostly from Steuben County to the north where Singleman had once been the power in the land.

Midday was the time he took his daytime nap. He would rise at mid-afternoon, his activities from there on dictated by his schedule. He might visit one of his many women, go drinking and carousing at one-horse Paloverde back in the hills, or maybe hunt wolf and puma across the Flintlocks — he was an excellent shot. One day was never the same as another, he was always fully occupied and never truly alone. At any time day or night there were always men with guns within call.

Singleman had land, money, investments and cash reserves. But where he was really rich, was in enemies, even if some of those enemies might tell you they weren't really sure if he existed or not anymore.

A full year ago now, having barely evaded a five-year stretch in Sabbatch

Jail on a charge of political conspiracy — a sentence since reversed by his influential associates in Steuben County — the power-broker had sought and secured his hideaway in the remote Wigfall Breaks region beyond Tumbleweed Valley south of Rivertown.

Staff, gunmen, underlings and business associates were forbidden to mention his name either here or elsewhere. The occasional transgressor in this regard was 'disappeared', a technique Singleman had perfected over time. He rarely visited Rivertown and only a handful of trusted aides ever knew exactly where he was, where he'd been, where he might be going next.

He enjoyed hearing the stories where people swore they'd sighted him someplace he'd never been, had attended his funeral or had a female relative who was one of his mistresses.

Although active in various criminal activities in the region, Singleman was in essence a man enduring self-imposed exile before the day he would return to his former world of politics, power and the machinery of government.

In Steuben County.

It had been in that remote quarter that the one-time power-broker had enjoyed his greatest successes as founder and driving force of the semi-legitimate and eventually highly influential organization known as the Steuben County Citizens Committee, a conservative title that helped conceal its true precepts and goals.

Power was what Singleman had sought and all but achieved in his heyday in the north. With the assistance and complicity of a crooked circuit judge, paid stooges and informants in Salt Lake City supported by his armed riders and enforcers, he might have gone on to secure full legitimate control of remote Steuben, with his stooges occupying the County Commissioner's chair and other allies installed in positions of power and responsibility, but for the militia.

Colonel Palmer and his militiamen

had exerted a mainly benign authority — supported unofficially by a territorial government that lacked the will and resources to administrate the remote and turbulent Steuben County properly — and continued to enjoy the support and loyalty of the county that it had saved almost single-handedly from the enemy during the Civil War.

When Singleman's rampant ambition eventually clashed with the militia's concept of what was best for the county, and ultimately, with the militia itself, a shocked, chastened and imper-illed Singleman came off second best and was forced to quit the county to avoid arrest on charges of vote-rigging and interfering with due process, along with other charges.

That clash had enshrined the militia in a unique position of power, which it had enjoyed to this day.

But ever since the overthrow of the Citizens' Committee, Singleman had been quietly but relentlessly patching fences, renewing old contacts, playing host to men of influence in northern affairs, convincing just as many people as he could that he'd learned his lesson and would prove himself to be the man capable of leading the county to wealth and power upon his return.

But today, for once, Singleman felt free of his usual concerns and uncertainties as he made his way through to the front entrance of the old Rosedale Ranch headquarters.

The reason for his high spirits were simple. After far too long in self-imposed exile, of plotting, planning and scheming for his return, he had quite suddenly sighted an opportunity to strike a potentially fatal blow against his enemies, the militia, and with scarcely a hitch had succeeded. Who wouldn't feel good now that he could envision the end of self-imposed exile and the full resumption of his interrupted career in the north?

His hour of resurrection was at hand.

He headed outside.

The man who went light-footed

down the stone steps to the enclosed courtyard stood six feet three inches in stockinged feet. Powerful shoulders, a lumberjack's physique. His thick long hair was jet black whereas it had once been an undistinguished ginger-brown, and short. There were no photographs extant of how he appeared now and had done ever since coming south. There was nothing that could be done to disguise his size in the interests of anonymity, however. He'd tried walking with a stoop to minimize his height but realized he was too vain for that so had adopted other measures.

He was a man of extreme strengths and weaknesses. He had no close friends and didn't miss them a bit. He had his wide range of criminal interests, any number of loyal gunmen-bodyguards here and one family member living. He was content but for the hunger in his guts. That would never be appeased until he was back where he belonged, manipulating the strings controlling his political stooges in one of the most potentially prosperous and powerful regions on the frontier.

He nodded in approval as he glanced around the compound to see signs of unusual activity on every hand, where customarily the yard and outbuildings would be quiet and orderly this time of day.

Wagons were being loaded, goods and boxes emerging from indoors for stacking and loading. The penultimate phase of his planning and decisive action was at hand.

He crossed the courtyard and entered the barn, which doubled as shooting range. A man waited with his favorite gun, a long-barreled Peacemaker Colt. The weapon was armed with six soft-nosed bullets that were of low-pressure make to reduce recoil.

Such a weapon armed in this way was next door to ineffective at anything but close range. That was how he wanted it. Close range. If ever some bounty killer, lawdog or just some gunpacking fool should somehow get the jump on him one day, Singleman wanted in his fist something that would blast huge crimson holes in head, chest and guts at close quarters. He'd used it just once in such a situation during a buffalo hunt out in Nevada one hair-raising night. He emerged unharmed. The dry-gulcher was buried in a closed coffin; not even his kin had wanted to see what the Peacemaker had done to his face.

Holding the weapon before him he hammered six methodical shots into the paper bullseye thirty feet away. The attendant wound the target up for his inspection. Four bulls out of six. Good enough.

Breakfast called. It was an unusual day in every way but he would adhere to his routine.

Casey Hatch was awaiting his arrival at the top of the steps leading into the morning room. The gunman with the hatchet face wore black with a brown duster that reached to his knees. The man amused Singleman with his vanity and posturing, although there wasn't one single element of humor in the man himself.

Hatch had been with him ever since his early days, had been the man in charge of their recent and daring operation up at Placerville.

As Singleman nodded he noted the crêpe armband on the upper right sleeve of the brown duster.

'Donovan?' he guessed.

'Yes, boss.'

'You and him were kind of buddies, weren't you?'

'He was the best. Now he's dead, cut off in his prime by those tenth-rater scum off of the Dixie Belle.'

'I'm not sure they're tenth-raters from what I hear.'

'Whatever you say, Mr Singleman.'

Singleman glanced around at the activity. 'Well, all going to plan by the look of it.'

'Ready to roll by sundown I reckon.'

'Well, keep at it and make sure

nobody slacks off. Has my party arrived yet?'

'Came in overnight.'

'Good. Go tell them I'll be there in an hour.'

Halfway through the doorway, he paused. His eyes flickered over the familiar landscape of timbered hills and wintry rangeland beyond the high fence enclosing the home twenty acres.

Rosedale Ranch was as remote as it was possible to get in the rugged, mainly useless country south of Tumbleweed Valley. Its remoteness and the vigilance of the Singleman gunmen guaranteed its total privacy.

'Anything unusual?' he asked.

The gunslinger shook his head. 'Not so far leastways, sir. That's if you're referring to Placerville?'

'Of course I am. Still, everything went like clockwork and we covered our tracks as efficiently as always.' Singleman nodded. 'All right, on your way.'

He watched the man cross the courtyard with his familiar lithe step.

Hatch was not a big man. He was the bantam cock of the Rosedale and by far the most dangerous man there, apart from his employer.

Singleman ate a simple meal at an elaborately ornamented table of solid crystal.

'Only myself for breakfast?' he asked the Chinese servant who served him.

'Yes, Master.'

Singleman's jaws stopped rotating, then moved again. The salmon was first class and he washed it down with a beautiful red. Once imprisoned in his early days, where breakfast had been a bowl of gruel and chunk of salt bread, he'd vowed to breakfast well always thereafter.

Hatch was waiting for him again when he emerged following coffee and a long cigar. From after sunrise onwards, as it was now, he never moved outside the house without at least one shootist at his side. Few people were even aware that the old ranch was occupied again. Those who knew or suspected it to be the headquarters of a notorious figure in Utah power politics, were even fewer.

In the time he'd lived here there had been but a single incident. One summer midnight, men in dark garb carrying guns had come over a wall at the back of the stables and made it all the way into the house itself before the alarm was raised. Rosedale lost three men in the fierce gun battle that ensued, but the intruders were decimated by Hatch's men with only one surviving to be questioned by Singleman.

He was amused to discover that the man who'd sent the killers in was not a victim of one of his many operations, as he'd at first suspected, but merely the outraged husband of a woman he'd seduced.

He'd had him pegged out under the summer sun where it took ants, sun, thirst and blood loss three full days to finish him off. This was a warning to any others who might entertain notions of coming against him.

Towering over his gunman, Single-man glanced over his head in the direction of the squat red brick building referred to as the gymnasium. He cocked his head but failed to detect the familiar chinking of metal weights or the dull thud of heavy objects hitting the reinforced flooring.

'Probably sleeping in, sir,' Hatch said, catching his look. 'He was up late last night.'

Singleman just nodded and they continued on to the converted stables. It had been a barn but was now a prison. Trotter guarded the doors. The gunman moved smartly to shoot the lock and swing the side door open, saluting with his free hand as the two ducked their heads and went through.

They found the hostage pacing up and down the center of the gloomy, high-walled room, hands locked behind his back, chin held high like he was reviewing a ride-past of the Steuben County Militia.

The colonel halted abruptly as

Singleman came down a single step and approached. The prisoner was aware he was in the deepest trouble of his life-time but his spirit remained intact.

'Come to gloat, Singleman? Or perhaps it's time for the *coup de grâce*?'

'I certainly didn't go to all the trouble of netting you just to snuff you out, Colonel. That would be foolish and I'm anything but a foolish man.'

'Anything but a man, don't you mean, sir?'

Singleman's smile was smooth as he moved in a wide circle around his prisoner, looking him up and down as though evaluating his exact worth.

'You must be curious to know what this is all about, Colonel?'

'Why, sir, I already know. It's about devilment, crime and evil. You vermin may imagine you are clever, complex and daring, but when it's all boiled down you're as predictable as the sunrise. You either plan to ransom me or hope to extract information from me on any number of important matters I may or may not be privy too. Well, my coffers are anything but healthy, which will find you disappointed if it's extortion, while on the second issue you won't get anything out of me under duress. Far better men than you have tried.'

'Oh, you'll talk, Colonel. After a while you'll beg to talk — when I'm ready to listen.' Singleman was suddenly curt. 'All right, Hatch, the door. I'm running late for an appointment.'

'I'll see you publicly hanged in Steuben County!' Palmer shouted after him. 'That's a promise, and a Palmer never breaks his word.'

The big man genuinely did have an appointment. His guests were assembled in the map room when he arrived a short time later.

Not one of those present resembled a crook, outlaw, shyster or crooked politician. Well-dressed and showing good manners as they greeted their host, they might have been a distinguished grouping of civic leaders, successful businessmen or simply and proudly gentlemen of importance in the bustling and booming West of the 1870s.

They were nothing of the kind. Each one was an opportunist cum conspirator bent on shaping Utah their way, while they in turn recognized him as the only man capable of leading and guiding them to that heady goal.

They had the ambition; Singleman could supply the engine power to drive it. The big man had just reaffirmed his worth and daring with the abduction of Colonel Palmer and over the following two hours, he had them eating out of the palm of his hand.

He was watching them leave under a pallid midday sun when he heard the familiar sound coming from the direction of the gymnasium. It was the dull thud of a heavy weight hitting the floor.

He nodded and smiled and knew all was well with his world.

7

Bounty Man

The riders came in slowly across the wide green sweeps of Wasach Pass along a trail that provided the only easy access for any westbounder traveling this route for the minefields and free lands beyond.

Seven in number and well mounted on good horseflesh, the graying senior riders of the Steuben County Militia always rode with pride in their outfit here, as they had the right. Several years ago, when the verdant mile-wide strip of the pass had been first sighted and quickly settled by the first straggle of migrants surging west after the war, the militiamen had been foremost amongst those welcoming the newcomers and were happy to see them take this easy, unofficial route through the pass rather than be forced to resort to the rough tracks through the ranges of the Purple Mountains, rearing on either side.

All that changed when gold was struck due west and the government threw the Indian lands open to free settlement. Overnight the human trickle became a flood and the prime Wasach Pass grazelands threatened to disintegrate into a single torn and muddy trail endangering the survival of some twenty to thirty of the finest rancher settlements in the region.

The settlers rebelled against the intrusion but the flood kept on coming. There was destruction, violence, several deaths. The army came in once but refused to open fire on their fellow Americans and quickly departed for the comparative quiet of the Indian wars.

When Colonel Palmer had ridden away from Steuben County with his militia to assist at the goldfields, the pass had been an almost idealized representation of what the Great West could become now the vital ingredient of people was being added.

He returned to disaster and was enraged, having long believed that, rightly or wrongly, the Steuben County he'd helped save from the enemy in the war was his personal responsibility.

With influence in high places in the distant capital he contacted Salt Lake City and begged for assistance to help control the rampaging human flood.

His request was denied — with regrets.

Governmental resources were stretched too thinly, he was advised. There was more in the same negative vein emanating from the governor's office, but almost at the end of the letter came a suggestion, nothing stronger than that, that 'perhaps the militia might be able to lend some assistance personally to stabilize the situation.'

The colonel had been dealing with officialdom, the army, the lawmen and the law itself in his isolated corner of the territory long enough to realize that he was, in an offhanded unofficial way, being extended authority far beyond his ranking to deal with difficult situations himself, should he so choose.

He so chose.

When the No Trespass signs reappeared this time, fifty militiamen appeared alongside them, armed and mounted, almost as rugged, determined and flinty-looking as they had been fifteen years ago when they had gone to war. There were skirmishes and several woundings followed a week or so of high tension while the migrants grew accustomed to the idea that the pass genuinely was shut off, and that was the end of it. The Conestogas and handcarts, the wheelbarrows and spring-wheeled buggies, travois and the trudging lines of people afoot returned to the old roundabout way through the Purples and had been doing so ever since — yet another victory to the colonel and his militia.

From that day on the militia had been left to provide the strength and security that the government simply could not supply, and apart from the ongoing conflict against their long-standing enemies of the Syndicate, Steuben County had run smoothly and peacefully ever since.

Yet captain and retinue appeared anything but victorious that day as they entered the plank-bar section of the General Store, the combination store, saloon and livery that formed the centerpiece of the tiny village of Hopeville that serviced the landhold-ers.

The evil news had hit like a thunderclap the previous day. Few of the militiamen leaders present had slept since.

'We could get on down there,' one man suggested after a weighty silence.

'And do what?' snapped the captain. 'Ride in like a bunch of cowboys and shoot up the place?'

'Heck, I didn't mean that, Captain — '

'I should hope not.' The captain took a swig and stared dully out the door. He added wistfully. 'We might've done just that and gotten away with it ten years ago, but . . . ' His voice trailed away.

'I suppose,' offered another veteran after a silence, 'that if we were to be truthful with each other, none of us could honestly say what happened to the colonel was anything but overdue.' He met their stares and spread his hands. 'I mean — think about it. The colonel was never one for shying away from trouble, like pretty women, big games, even fist fights with fellers half his age. We've bailed him out a dozen times ourselves — '

'For God's sake, man!' the captain broke in. 'You're talking about a few harmless scrapes. The man has been kidnapped, maybe dead already. You saying he deserved that?'

That shut the veteran up smartly. Another round was ordered, a deeper silence descended. The militiamen were men of action, accustomed to the clear-headed leadership of their colonel in times of crisis. Today they were on their own and it didn't feel good.

'You know,' a veteran with silver mustache and goatee said finally, brightening up some, 'you realize we're just going on newspaper talk and hen-scratch gossip here. We all know how these things can get exaggerated, blown all out of shape. Instead of sitting here fretting about what we'd do without him, or moon-shining about riding south, why don't we wait until they make it official? If it's still bad news then, we'll handle it. But I've a feeling it could prove better than we expect.'

Heads nodded, backs straightened. Maybe Cody is right. Let's have another and think positive.

The gloom lifted until some time later when the store clerk came through clutching a manila envelope.

'Captain Parmenter,' he said. 'Just come for you.'

A sudden silence. Hesitant now, the captain took the envelope, stared at it. 'Post-marked Rivertown,' he said in a husky voice.

They crowded around. He ripped it open and something fell to the floor. One picked it up. They recognized the object at once. It was a medal Colonel Palmer had been awarded at the war's end in acknowledgement of the militia's services.

There was a note. The captain cleared his throat and read:

'Commander, Steuben County Militia.

Colonel Palmer is now our prisoner in the war against entrenched corruption in your region as exemplified by the militia, the legislative corps and the venal officers of government and law.

Militia to be disbanded and quit Steuben County upon receipt of this communication otherwise the corrupt life of Palmer the traitor and false authority will be immediately forfeit.

Signed,

The Syndicate.'

The reader appeared to have aged ten years as he looked up. The Syndicate represented the shadowy political forces of Steuben County arraigned against the incumbent administration. There had been bad blood and sporadic conflict between the strong-arm faction of the Syndicate and the militia over several years, which had occasionally resulted in murder, law suits and ever increasing tension. The Democrats supported by the militia were in and the Syndicate-backed opposition seemed permanently out — unless all that had suddenly changed with this brief letter.

Not a man spoke. What was there to say when confronted by the unthinkable?

Cole Vallantry sat in his shirt-sleeves with his three-legged stool tilted back against the wall of the hotel porch and boot-tips just reaching the floor, cleaning his sixshooter. Pushing the oily rag through the barrel with the cleaning rod, he forced it through time after time and held the muzzle to his eye to peer along the dark mirror shine of the barrel. He tested the action and replaced the weapon in its holster, then reached for his drink.

The cook appeared in the doorway from the dining-room wearing a flour-dusted apron and an amiable grin. From behind the man came the aromatic drift of bacon and eggs and hot coffee.

'Breakfast's as good as ready, young feller.'

'And so am I, Billy boy.'

In truth, Vallantry was even more than simply ready to eat, he reflected as he toed his possibles bag out of his way on the floor and got to his feet. It was nine in the morning and for most of the past twelve hours he'd been searching all over — here in Rivertown, its slumtown and out in the quarter-acre farmlets immediately beyond, then the open range-lands proper to east, west and south.

He'd questioned scores of people, drawing the same response every single time. Shaking heads. Nobody had seen anything of a fifty-six-year-old gentleman known even this far south of his homeland as the colonel, although virtually all had heard about the kidnapping by now.

Occasionally during his questioning he'd casually dropped the name of Singleman, only to be met with blank stares in every case.

Disappointing. But he could live with that. If this breakfast tasted as good as it smelt he'd be ready to start afresh again in an hour.

The cook vanished and Cole turned his head as his brother walked into sight beyond the stables. He could see by his heavy tread that Buck also was one weary searcher. His expression further suggested that he had also failed to be crowned by success, which was confirmed when Buck mounted the porch, tugged off his sweat-stained sombrero and shook his head.

'Nobody knows anything, saw anything or wants to talk about anything.' He sniffed. 'Say, I hope that's chow I smell.'

'Fresh, hot and ready.' Cole rested hands on hips and squinted at the glare coming off the streets. 'Seen Lauren today?'

Buck leaned against the wall. 'Stopped by the hotel. She's holding up OK, I guess.'

'You know, I'm getting a feeling this town really doesn't know anything, like it says.'

'Same here. But we still know they headed west from Placerville. And we haven't found that rubber-tyred coach yet.'

'Sounds like you're saying this means we've got to comb the entire countryside, just two of us.' Cole massaged his jaw, clean-shaven as always. 'And I guess two will be the best we can do. These people act like they couldn't care less about a man of distinction being snatched off the streets, plus a man killed in the affair.'

'Speaking of that. There's a full story on what happened in Placerville including Slick Donovan getting killed. You and I get a mention.'

Cole smiled humorlessly. 'I sensed I was drawing the odd hostile stare. But then that's nothing new for me.'

Buck grunted and pushed off the wall, heading for the kitchen doorway. Weary-footed, he kicked Cole's bag, upsetting it. He bent to right it and the poster fell out. He picked it up, was about to replace it when he realized it was a black-and-white wanted dodger with the pen portrait of a dark-faced powerful looking man portrayed above the blazing words:

WANTED
NICHOLAS SINGLEMAN
MURDER
&
BLACKMAIL
TEN THOUSAND DOLLARS
DEAD OR ALIVE
SHERIFF'S OFFICE,
PALOVERDE CITY, COLORADO.

'Give me that!' Cole snapped, snatching the poster from his fingers. He thrust it back in the valise and closed it. But it was too late. Buck had seen what he'd seen. His face was pale.

'Working for the government you claim?' he said bitterly. 'Buffalo dust! You're hunting this feller for the money. You're a bounty hunter.' He turned his head and spat.

For a moment it seemed Cole would deny it. Then a hard glitter of pride came to his eye, he lifted his chin and spoke calmly, unrepentantly.

'Bounty hunter and proud of it, cowboy. You make your living tromping through horse-dung, I make mine bringing in bloody-handed butchers the law can't catch. What's the difference? It's a living — '

'Just a minute. All the work you've been putting in here since the kidnapping — it wasn't for Lauren or the colonel, was it? You were just backing a hunch that a big-time crook, like this Singleman has to be — and who just might have been seen that night up at Placerville — might turn out to be the crook with enough guts and manpower to grab the biggest man in Steuben County. That's it, ain't it?'

'I've a hunch our bacon and eggs might be getting cold.'

'So, you don't deny what I say?'

'If Singleman did snatch Palmer and we nail him for it and save the colonel's hide, what the hell does it matter who's done what for whatever reason?' Cole spread his hands. 'The good side wins. Isn't that what life's supposed to be all about?'

He swung and vanished through the

doorway. At the end of a long minute, Buck shook his head and followed.

An hour later saw them quit the hotel together and make for the livery. They weren't talking, but they weren't ruckusing any longer either. There was a job to be done. The unspoken understanding appeared to be — get the job done and worry about their differences later.

★   ★   ★

He took no part in the unusual bustle of activity around the inner compound that morning.

He stood on the top step of the front balustrade, the house rearing behind him and wan sunlight dappling the hills of the estate beyond the walls as servants went to and from the house to the stables toting luggage and boxed goods.

His dress was black. Flat-brimmed hat tugged low to shadow the eyes. Tight-fitting shirt and twin guns buckled low. A black armband circled the sleeve of the brown duster that reached to his knees.

The complete man of the gun but for one thing. Casey Hatch was simmering with anger, and anger could be dangerous for a man of his caliber. It could interfere with his judgment, make a man act impulsively when he should be calm and steady. Anger was for amateurs.

A servant staggered down the steps lugging a satchel of documents. Singleman's records, letters and data from his halcyon days as power-broker up in Steuben County's wild days, before he was forced to leave. The papers would be returning north with Singleman. Everything was changing up there. The big man was waiting for a reply wire from the militiamen re his hostage.

Hatch was also eager for the return north, but hated the notion of leaving unfinished business behind.

A door creaked below and a young man emerged from the brick building that stood by the stables. His eyes narrowed as he focused upon the Herculean shape of David Singleman, standing there blinking in the sunlight.

The lean and lethal gunpackers of the spread often referred to Single-man's son as 'dummy' or 'the block'. But never where they might be overheard. Singleman was anything but an affectionate man, yet was protective concerning his retarded son to an almost obsessive degree.

Hatch sneered at that thought. He knew why the big man felt and acted that way. It wasn't love, but guilt.

He knew the man would head toward the cement blocks lined up by the south wall, the blocks with steel handles set in their upper side.

David Singleman was massively built as a result of years spent doing the only thing that interested him since 'the accident'. Testing his strength against heavy objects, sometimes outside but mostly in the solid building where he lived and slept alone but for the company of dumb-bells, bars loaded up with heavy steel discs, swings suspended from the roof and a great heavy canvas bag suspended from a cross-beam and stuffed tight with padding, which you'd sometimes hear him pounding, pounding with huge fists long into the night.

Hatch watched the young man seize the handles of two blocks and slowly raise them from the ground until he could straighten his back. The gunman had tested himself on one of the weights once. It felt like they were anchored to the core of the earth.

He felt like sneering but couldn't do it right. His mind was far away, in Rivertown. Then it jumped farther to Placerville's dreary Boot Hill.

He would admit Slick Donovan hadn't been much of either a player or a man, but when your bloody reputation and arrogance alienated most everybody a man came in contact with, the very few friends you could claim assumed a disproportionate significance.

A familiar voice sounded from the

balcony directly above. 'Morning, son.' No mistaking Singleman's deep tones.

The young man gazed up, nodded, returned to his blocks. Hatch stepped back to avoid being seen should the boss man lean over to see where he was. When he heard Singleman quit the balcony he licked dry lips and danced lightly down the steps to head for the stables.

He had no firm plans, he told himself. Only knew he would ride into Rivertown and maybe have a few drinks and catch up with the wagons when they crossed the river bridge. He'd take a look around that man's town. Donovan would not expect him to do anything less.

8

Raging Guns

'I'm right sorry, Miss Palmer, but there's no ways ladies is allowed in the bath house.'

'What if I insist on going in?' came the imperious reply.

The bath house proprietor blinked uncomprehendingly. Females avoided his establishment like the plague, as they rightly should. Maybe if a girl from Maisie's came along, full of gin and looking for her no-account man, he might understand even if he still wouldn't allow her inside. But this was the colonel's daughter and without doubt the new darling of the town, what with her looks and charm and all that she was going through.

He opened his mouth to explain further but Lauren suddenly couldn't maintain her serious pose any longer. She laughed.

'It's all right, Mr Timkins, I was only funning.' She sobered. 'But I would be obliged if you would inform the Mr Vallantrys that I'd like them to join me at the Collins House for refreshments, if you would be so kind?'

'Count on me, Missy. And . . . and is there any news . . . ?'

'None, I'm afraid.'

'Well, you keep your chin up.' The man jerked a thumb over his shoulders. 'These two jaspers are doing their durndest to turn up something. Could hardly walk they were so beat when they rode back to town.'

It was true. Their frustration mounting by the hour, the searchers had combed the lands south of the river until their horses simply gave up on them. And all for nothing. They'd shown up at the bathhouse grim, unshaven and bone-weary, yet none of this showed when they stepped outside a short time later and headed down the wide, tree-lined main stem.

'I knew we needed something, but didn't know what it was until old hairy-face told us she wanted to see us,' Buck grinned. Then he sobered. 'Only wish we had some news for her.'

'No news today. Perhaps there's not going to be any news any day. My experience with these sorts of crimes suggests that the longer they drag on the less likely the victim is to survive.'

'You've worked on kidnappings before?' His brother's choice of a mid-thirties career still had Buck Vallantry baffled.

'Not really. But I've met men who have. Of course the positive aspect in this case is that Palmer was obviously abducted for a purpose. We know he's highly prominent up north, a man of authority with an unusual amount of power and influence, or at least that's how you paint him. A kidnapper would have every good reason to want to keep the man alive until he'd at least got what he wanted out of him. After that I wouldn't give a snap for his chances, so we'd better turn up something soon before his time runs out.'

'You aiming to tell Lauren all that?'

'Of course not. I'll lie.'

The Collins House was big and airy with white linen tablecloths, good silver and even flowers on the tables.

Lauren looked lovely, no sign of red eyes. They ordered coffee and as good as his word, Cole spun a tale on how they were working on some strong leads and should be able to expect results in the not too distant future.

Buck sat back and let his brother talk. He was still disappointed about the bounty hunting, but wisely let it ride. In truth he was too preoccupied with their hunt for the missing man to have much time left over to fret about anything, including the wild horse season, slowly passing by down south.

They noticed the girl wasn't drinking. They could hardly be surprised.

'These leads you mention,' she said. 'What is the strongest one you're working on?'

They traded glances. Buck smiled easily. 'The coach, Lauren,' he said, then nodded emphatically. 'Yeah, that's our best. You see, this rig we're looking for, we know it's big, likely cost a whole heap, even has rubber-tired wheels. It's hard to hide a vehicle like that, or at least not have folks see it.'

Cole was ready to change the subject. 'While we have you with us, Lauren, could you tell us a little more about Steuben County, what your life's been like up there, the general set-up involving your father. The more we know the better our chances of drawing up a composite picture.'

Buck snorted at that. Sometimes he was convinced Cole's tongue-twisters were made up. Composite! That sounded like a poultice they made up for you when you came down with the ague.

An hour passed pleasantly and it was late afternoon when they dropped Lauren off at her hotel and stopped off at the law office.

The lawman had no new information

and gave the clear impression this didn't worry him overly. He had a big town to run and Placerville's concerns weren't his. They mentioned the coach but the man looked blank. He might have been a wizard at keeping cowboys from riding their prads up onto the plankwalks when full of rye, but major crime didn't seem his cup of tea.

There was no presentiment of danger as they strolled through the gathering dusk, laying tomorrow's plans. Lovers were strolling, thirsty citizens were heading for the bars and a steady stream of traffic flowed up and down the length of main.

They felt the weariness begin to hit again as they took a table in the dining annex off the main bar room of the Dollar King Saloon. They ordered steaks and were about through with their first drinks when Buck broke off what he was saying and cocked his head.

'What?' Cole said.

'Listen.'

Cole looked around. He could hear a roulette wheel spinning, a girl's sudden shrill laughter, the diminishing murmur of sound from the room beyond the wide archway.

He sharpened. That was it! The bar room had been noisy when they passed through it to the annex. Now the noise was down by half, still falling.

Their eyes locked and they were pushing to their feet when the voice reached them.

'Well, looky here. The federal marshals, ain't it? Uh huh, could only be, judging by all the snooping and quizzing going on. Funny thing though, when you come to take a look at 'em, they don't exactly look like lawmen, do they, Clem? More like . . . what's the word I'm looking for? Oh yeah. More like buttinskers, wouldn't you say?'

Both were on their feet by this. He stood leaning in the doorway, the bar now totally quiet behind him.

The man was below medium height dressed in dark, tight rig under a long brown duster. The face was pale, broad-boned and intense with hollows accentuating gaunt cheekbones. He wore two guns and despite his even tone and semi-relaxed stance, radiated an electric kind of tension.

'Who the hell are you?' Buck's tone was rough-edged. The days had been hard and exhaustion had only been deferred, not eliminated. Someone stood behind the man in black, beyond them the now hushed and gaping bar room.

'Hatch,' came the level reply. A pause. 'Casey Hatch.'

'If that's supposed to mean something to us, it doesn't,' said Cole.

Twin spots of pink touched Hatch's cheekbones. Pushing his shoulder off the doorjamb, he came into the room with a slouching, silky walk. The man radiated self-assurance. His manner was hostile yet he seemed to be holding himself under control.

'Donovan was a pard of mine — if that means anything to you,' he snapped, halting with knees snapped back, hands resting on hips. He nodded. 'Yeah, I can see it does.'

'He tried to kill us and we killed him.' Cole's tone was neutral. He was trying to figure if Casey Hatch had trouble in mind, or whether he just wanted to get something off his chest.

So was Hatch. He wanted some kind of redress yet was momentarily wary of going too far. The newcomers looked likely at close range, more so than he'd expected.

'He was a good man,' he stated.

'He was a crook, a would-be killer and maybe a kidnapper,' Buck retorted.

Hatch stiffened. 'Kidnapper?' he said warily. 'What are we talking about here?'

'We're investigating the abduction by force of Colonel Palmer from Steuben County,' Cole stated. 'Would you know anything about that, Hatch?'

It was a shot in the dark but hit home. Hatch backed up a step, all nonchalance adrift now.

'Just who the hell are you? Some kind of law?'

'Concerned citizens,' said Cole. 'Where do you think you're going?'

Hatch was heading for the exit. Not scared, just suddenly unsure of exactly what he was up against. Cool-headed, he may have made it all the way through the archway and out of the saloon unhindered. But he was far from calm, smarting at the feeling he'd come off second best in the clash he'd called against the strangers, with scores lining the long bar straining their eyes to see what was going on, ears flapping.

'Shit, Casey,' slurred his sidekick, Clem, as he reached the doorway, 'you gonna let these chittlewits climb all over you that ways — after what they done to poor Donovan?'

The gunman propped, staring at the man who also rode for Singleman. By breakfast everybody out there would know that Singleman's top gun had let a couple of nobodies shame him in front of the whole saloon.

181

He whirled and pointed.

'We don't welcome your kind here. I'll give you time to saddle up and check out, then . . . '

'Then what?' Buck growled as his voice faded.

'Then I'll hunt you out.' Hatch slapped gunbutt. 'With this.'

The Vallantrys traded looks. They might have gone on with it but saw no point. Certainly they'd be checking up on Casey Hatch to see if the man might measure up to anything significant. But they didn't want to get into any kind of scrape with the man here; they had troubles enough without that.

'Whatever you say,' Cole said placatingly.

'Yeah . . . what he says,' Buck added offhandedly.

But Singleman's man suddenly wasn't about to be appeased. He imagined he caught a whiff of weakness, and that was enough for him to realize he could take hold of this situation and come out on top.

'Looks like you've overplayed your hands,' he said icily. He nodded. 'So that means the rules have changed.' He jerked a thumb over his shoulder. 'I've decided you're leaving, and right now. Out of here, out of town, out of our lives. Vamoose, high-steppers.'

Quiet before, suddenly the saloon fell totally silent. Shaking his head, Cole took a step toward the man who had slipped into a menacing stance, right hand above gunbutt, a fast gun poseur.

'Look, Hatch, why don't we — '

'Drop your guns and git!'

Cole dropped hand to gun handle, aware of his brother fanning out to his side. Hatch's eyes were crazy and there was the sensation of teetering on the edge of a high cliff as the seconds screamed by.

The man cursed and went for his gun.

Buck's draw and clear was fast but his brother was faster. Cole's Colt erupted in an ear-slamming crack of sound that set the bar room glasses tinkling.

Instantly the gunman was flung back with white-hot death engulfing him. He squeezed his trigger unaimed, the shot hammering floorboards between his boots. Lost in a totality of deafening sound, the man sought desperately to grin in final defiance as he lurched toward the motionless figure wreathed in gunsmoke. He fell forward onto the boards. He felt a hand on his back. Clem spoke but he didn't hear. He tried to speak but choked on blood.

★   ★   ★

The sheriff kept writing while Buck Vallantry kept speaking. Cole said nothing, standing by the window with arms folded, face gaunt and pale in the lamplight.

'. . . And the assumed reason behind Mr Hatch's attack, Mr Vallantry?'

'We gunned down his friend up at Placerville. Guess he was sore about that.'

The pen scratched until Cole's

sudden voice blotted it out.

'Where did Hatch come from? Nobody seems sure.'

The lawman massaged the back of his neck. 'Well, from down south some, I guess . . .'

'You only guess? Don't you know? He's known hereabouts.'

Cole was tense, aggressive. The bloody business at the saloon had appeared so pointless. He'd come out alive but it didn't feel like any kind of victory.

'Well . . .' the lawman said for a second time, and Cole snatched up his hat.

'That settles it. We'll go find the one that ran off — Clem, whatever his name is. He'll tell us and maybe throw some light on all this.'

'All right, all right,' the law said appeasingly. 'No call to do that and mebbe see more blood spilled. We believe Hatch and Clem both rode for an old place someone took over about a year back. It's about twenty miles south

185

along Cache Creek in what they call the Wigfall Breaks region. Rosedale Ranch, it used to be called. But I'd be kinda cautious if you're thinking of going down there. Them folks ain't entirely hospitable, if I hear right.'

'We won't be looking for hospitality, just answers,' Cole snapped, striding for the door. 'Coming or not?'

'Heck,' Buck sighed, flipping his hat and catching it. 'Coming . . . I guess.'

*   *   *

The first cold light of dawn stippled the weeping trees and tinted the rain puddles. They stood side by side in the compound yard listening to the rain on the roof. Each man held a cocked .45 in his fist as he allowed his gaze to play over the wide and empty yard, the silent outbuildings, the iron-roofed house where no early morning smoke rose from twin chimneys.

'Deserted or a trap?' Cole wondered aloud.

186

'Cover me and I'll find out.'

'Where are you going?'

'Check the house first.'

'Damnit, I'll come with you.'

'You don't have to. Besides, this tells me there's nobody here.' He tapped the side of his nose with a finger.

'The wonder trailsman!'

Buck halted. 'Look, it's over. You shot him because he would have shot us. Let it go.'

'Easy for you to say,' Cole snapped, yet seemed less tense as they mounted the steps together and tested the front door. Unlocked.

They emerged several minutes later with guns pointing at the ground. The house was fully furnished but devoid of life. It had plainly only been recently vacated, possibly as recently as the previous day.

In turn they checked out the barns and outbuildings, eventually looked inside the square brick building standing alone. They stared in puzzlement at what they found, a small room containing a bunk, chair and table, the larger area cluttered with massive weights and exercise equipment.

But also empty.

Back under dripping skies they talked quietly, evaluating, guessing, speculating. From the very little they had been able to glean in town concerning Rosedale Ranch, the place had a secretive and even forbidding reputation; visitors were turned away by men with guns, nobody seemed quite sure who actually owned or rented the property although one or two connected it with the name of Singleman.

Hatch had been regarded as a gunman with a bad reputation. Several of his known associates, including the late Slick Donovan from up-river were also guntoters and highly secretive in their ways.

'Reckon they're coming back?' Cole asked after a silence.

Buck massaged the back of his neck. 'I've a hunch they ain't.'

'We'll have one last look about then

ride back to town.'

It was during the final survey of the compound that Buck came upon the clear print of a rubber-tired coach wheel in the mud. On the ride back to Rivertown, his scout's eyes picked out enough in the mixed, rain-affected road sign to convince him the coach, heavily laden, had travelled in to Rivertown, probably during the night.

By dark down the same day he'd detected the same sign on the north trail on the far side of the big river bridge below the town.

For the very first time that day, Cole showed some animation as they stood in the fast fading light staring north-wards.

'It's starting to make sense, cowboy.' He counted on his fingers. 'Palmer kidnapped, brought here, Hatch tries to kill us over Donovan. Now, Singleman — we have to believe it's him — has packed up with maybe a dozen men and all his gear and looks like he's heading north, maybe with the colonel, maybe not. What does that suggest to you?'

Buck liked to give conundrums careful thought. His eyes widened.

'We've been saying as how the militia might fold up north without the colonel leading them like always. We know Singleman damn near ran Steuben County once, might have done so but for the militia going against him.' His eyes widened. 'Are you figuring Single-man could be scheming to get back into the game up there using the colonel as a hostage, or something like?'

'Not 'or something',' Cole retorted. 'That has to be it. That makes sense of everything that's happened since Placer-ville, cowboy.'

'Then what are we doing standing here in the rain?'

They ran back to the horses across the big bridge.

9

Ridin' North

Shafter's Station, Mulberry River, the Contreras Plains and now one-horse Guber Wells. All slipped behind one after the other until now the cavalcade was rolling along the single-track trail where it cut across Fiftyfour Ranch with the McGraw Hills a faint blue line ahead.

It was still raining. That didn't prevent Singleman from occupying the high seat alongside the driver of the big coach. The big man was liberated both in body and spirit. Down south in exile he'd mostly traveled by night and always with armed outriders, never knowing when the law or someone with a grudge might show up through the tall and uncut with guns, wanted dodgers or evil intent.

He drank it all in, the big country under the vast gray skies, the four sturdy teamers in the harness, the sway and jolt of the big gleaming vehicle carrying him swiftly and proudly back over the same trail he'd followed southward one dark night, fearing he might never get to travel up it again.

'Here, give me that whip, Coughlin.'

The driver passed him the whip and Singleman reared up to his full height and cracked it just above the lead teamers' heads causing the pair to jump and roll their eyes backwards.

'Er, mebbe I wouldn't do that, Mr Singleman,' the driver warned. 'Don't want to end up in a ditch, do we, boss?'

The black-snake cracked again and again. Nobody told Singleman what to do on this of all days.

Inside the coach gunman McClure just grinned and glanced across at the hulking figure seated in the far corner. 'Don't recall ever seein' your old man in such high spirits, kid.'

There was no response. There never

was. David Singleman might have been watching the dreary countryside blurring by, or he may have been asleep with his eyes half-opened.

The trail dipped down into a low crossing and the mounted gunmen followed, splashing across.

Eight riders comprised the escort, which even Singleman might have conceded was not nearly enough number strength for a man bent on staging a coup. But for this journey the big man was not relying on numbers alone, but on his ace-in-the-hole travelling alone in the closed-in buggy with a gunman riding escort either side.

The colonel sat upright in the gloom of the rig, grunting each time the wheels hit a rut. Although Singleman had said nothing about his plans, he was certain he knew what they would be, just as he'd understood from the outset of his nightmare why he'd been abducted. The Free Lands Militia was his creation and he was the Free Lands Militia. He knew the men who'd ridden with him for so long, first in war and then in peace — or what passed for it west of the Mississippi.

If it became a decision between quitting the responsibility they'd discharged with such responsibility and success, and having his corpse dumped outside the General Store at Hopeville, he knew what their decision would be.

They would agree to disband and Singleman would be back where he had been before they'd thrown him out. He didn't doubt for a moment that the man had the ability, most probably the support in high places, and certainly the fire in his belly to grab up the reins of power as both of them — the colonel and the power-broker — had done in the past.

The rain let up abruptly and soon a feeble northern sun was shining. By dark down they would have crossed the border into Steuben County.

★   ★   ★

Captain Joe Dean was rubbing a little polish into the broad leather belt he always wore when representing the militia, when the knock sounded on the door of his modest three roomer in Hopeville, just along from the General Store.

The captain's hands went still. He was older than the colonel himself and the strain of the past ten days showed sharply in his lean face and the stoop of his shoulders.

He rose and went to the door. A stranger stood on the stoop, a youngish man who sported twin guns buckled around his middle beneath a grimed raincoat. He had a face like a wet knife blade and suddenly, instinctively, the captain knew, not who this was, but what.

The man's instinct for trouble was as sharp as it had been when the Free Lands Militia had fought for the county, and won.

An hour later he found himself standing in the front room of a sprawling ranch house several miles from Hopeville, a place he'd once vowed never to set foot in again due to the politics and aspirations of the rancher, Marshall Corben.

Corben was president of the Steuben County Citizens' Committee, longtime political opponents of the militia with influence in Salt Lake City, yet not enough to enable them to acquire local power in the county.

He'd not seen Corben smile in years but the big-nosed beanpole was smirking like the cat that ate the cream at the expression on Dean's face when a door opened and Singleman emerged, also smiling.

'You!' he gasped. He couldn't help it. 'What the hell do you think you're doing back here when — '

He broke off as a second figure appeared in the doorway. It was the colonel, his hands were tied and a young man with eyes like a snapping turtle held a pistol at his head.

In that moment Captain Joe Dean

knew that all his worst fears aroused by the colonel's abduction down south were realized.

★ ★ ★

The deputy governor scanned the yellow telegraph slip for about the dozenth time that morning as though hoping the contents might miraculously change. They didn't. The message was still brief, to the point and final.

His Honor, Deputy Governor Hale,
    To inform that as interim head of the Free Lands Militia I am tending the resignation of our commission, which will be regarded as accepted upon your receipt of this communication.
    Colonel Palmer and myself strongly recommend the installation of the Free Citizens' Committee as our only logical replacement.
    Respectfully yours,
    Captain Joseph Dean (retired).

Hale finally let the message drop to the blotter and leaned back wearily in his big heavy chair. He fingered the corners of his eyes and his adjutant studied him sympathetically.

'More trouble, sir. And now, of all times.'

'Of all times,' the tall man replied, swiveling his chair to stare dully at a map of the territory. The deputy governor was dedicated to his job even if the responsibility could be brutal at times. Utah was huge and sprawling and at times administration could be a nightmare. Steuben County, outlined in blue ink, was the most isolated and remote of all the counties and over the years Salt Lake City had been content to regard it as virtually self-reliant following a period of instability.

The sprinkle of capital personnel in the county could never have operated successfully down there without the commanding assistance of the Free Lands Militia, and the authorities only realized how vital that arrangement had proven after news reached the capital concerning Colonel Palmer's disappearance and possible death.

They'd learned of Singleman's return to the region only the previous day, now this. What the Sam Hill was going on down there?

'Shall I organize a deputation to travel down to Steuben and find out exactly what the situation is, sir?' the adjutant suggested.

'How I'd like to be in a position to authorize that,' Hale muttered. 'I should authorize it, but it's impossible with all we have on our plate.'

He swung the chair back to face the other, deep creases puckering his brow.

'Let's consider the situation calmly, Bob. Firstly, we always suspected that Singleman wasn't through down there even after the militia virtually booted him out. The man has never severed his contacts with important people in the administration and I know for a fact that many still regard him as the strong man we need down there, strong enough to run things with minimum involvement from us. Singleman is a bastard, nobody can argue with that. He's also a strong man in every sense of the word and God knows we don't have many of those sprinkled around the outlying regions, now do we?'

'I regard the man as a criminal, sir.'

'But a possible criminal who could at least keep the lid on Steuben until things improve here and we're able to deal with its problems more effectively?'

The adjutant had been put on the spot. The man fidgeted, rubbed the back of his neck, stared at the wall map, finally sighed.

'You're right, as always, sir. We simply don't have the resources necessary to send sufficient personnel to properly organize an election and soothe all the ruffled feathers. And, you know, I would bet my best boots that Singleman knew how tightly stretched we are before he made this play.'

'In all probability. We know only too well that he's kept all his lines of communication open with various high-ranking personnel here in government, who should know better.' He shook his head. 'Well, let's admit we'll probably regret making this decision, then you can draft a letter for my signature assuring them they'll have our support in the future providing they adhere strictly to all the principles for which this administration is famous — I don't think!'

'I'll attend to it right away, sir. I only hope we're doing the right thing.'

'Of course it's not the right thing, man. What we are doing is following the only course available under the circumstances, even if it proves to be the wrong thing.'

'Whatever you say, sir.'

* * *

It was late when the distant stutter of hoofbeats was heard by the last few night-owls still abroad in the quiet little town. A drinker at the General Store's back bar pricked his ears then took another slug, just in case.

Following several years of comparative peace in Steuben County, the past several days had been marked by shock, upheaval and deep concern over events that were unraveling at an astonishing rate for the little township and the closely settled rangeland surrounding it between the brooding jaws of the Purple Hills.

Out on the street itself, an insomniac sheepman was walking his woolly dog, but stepped into the shadows as the silhouette of two horsemen showed at the far end of the twisted main street and came slowly towards him.

Riders and horses looked weary, were. On his way north, their quarry had continually blotted their sign or laid down false trails in order to frustrate any pursuit from any quarter. Singleman had never seriously concerned pursuit might be a possibility but had been determined to ensure that he was given at least a few days to achieve his objectives and get his hands firmly back on the reins of power.

He was there already, as two weary and travel-stained riders discovered standing at the back-store bar downing stiff ones.

One of the night-owls happened to be a militiaman, or rather, as the man was quick to reveal bitterly, an ex-militiaman.

He gave it to them straight, just as they wanted it. The militia had resigned its commission, Singleman's gunmen and his long-time supporters, the Citizens' Committee, had bloodlessly taken over where they'd left off and there wasn't a damn thing anyone could do about it.

'Never mind all that guff,' a weary Buck Vallantry growled, rubbing his stubbled jaw. 'What about the colonel?'

The drinker shrugged and spread his hands.

'What can I tell you, gents? According to most everyone, the colonel's alive and in good fettle. And I know for a fact that was the case a few days back when Captain Dean was hauled up to face it out with Singleman. The captain allowed the colonel was looking a mite tired and strained, but very much alive. Guess there was no way the captain would've cancelled the militia's commission unless he was sure Colonel Palmer was alive and would be set loose as soon as it was done.'

A travel-stained Cole Vallantry pricked his ears. 'Then Palmer's free?'

The drinker shook his head.

'I said that's what Singleman promised to get him to set the wheels in motion. Ain't hide nor hair been seen of the colonel since. Knowing Singleman from the old days, some of us can't help wondering if we'll ever see him again. I mean, that bastard has got what he wants. Why would he keep alive a man who might get him hanged for kidnap somewhere down the track?'

'Why indeed?' Cole echoed as they prepared to bunk down at Joe Dean's three-roomer. He pulled off his shirt and reached for his cigars, staring across at Dean. 'Tell me, mister, do you think the man is dead and gone?'

'No,' came the unhesitating reply.

Cole drilled a look at Buck, slumped in a chair with one leg hooked over the arm. Buck immediately dropped his leg and sat up straighter. Now they were actually here in Steuben, each was aware that, badly as they might want to bring Singleman to book, the colonel was still their top priority.

'What makes you so sure?' Buck asked the captain.

The militiaman looked a little embarrassed. 'I guess mainly it's on account we always reckoned the colonel was, you know, immortal. Guess it was the way he took every fool risk in the book while we were fighting the Yankees that put the notion into our heads first.' He glanced at Buck, whom he knew by now was a lifetime Utahan. 'You know, places like Fort Glory, Tillerville . . . the Satchequaw Hills . . . '

The names of long ago battles stirred the big cowboy, bringing him to his feet. Maybe the captain had purposely invoked those names to fire him up. Maybe he'd succeeded.

'You know this country and its folk and we don't, captain. Say the colonel is still alive, where do you reckon a man should start in looking?'

'Just a moment, mister.' Cole had lit up and stood in characteristic pose, hands on hips, fuming stogie jutting from his teeth. 'Start looking, you say? Look, I was all for running that sonuva down and setting the colonel free out on the trail where we'd have still had upwards of a dozen gunpackers to deal with. We could have got ourselves killed, but I at least halfway thought it might be worth it. But by the sound of it the man's settled in here like he never left, he's got some sort of government support plus his own damned political machine. Can't you see what that adds up to?'

'You tell me,' Buck said harshly.

'Two dead brothers, that's what.'

'You're saying we should quit?'

'Well, not in so many words, maybe . . . '

'Then I guess they were right what they used say about you back home in the old days.'

Cole's eyes flared. He was a hard and probably selfish man, but he could be stung.

'And what would that be — brother?'

'That you were a quitter. That you quit on us when we were all young and poor . . . that you'd likely go on quitting all your life.'

'Those shrimps and losers said that?'

'All the time, mister, all the time.' Buck shrugged. 'And I guess they were right. Don't you agree?'

Cole Vallantry's lean and handsome face was blank. It was impossible to guess what was going on in his mind. He stared at his brother as though he hated him, but after a tense, slow time, he appeared to shake himself. He tugged the stogie from between his teeth.

'All right, all goddamned right!' He

began pacing round the room, cartridge-belt gleaming, jaw set hard. 'So, what if we stayed? What if I was fool enough to risk what's left of my life? What's in it for me?'

'You still might get Singleman and that ten grand he's worth in Colorado. Plus the satisfaction of doing something really worth while for once if we get to save Lauren's father. What do you say?'

Another long pause; there was no telling how Cole was thinking. 'I must be a damned fool . . . I never figured this would involve taking on the whole world!' He shook his head and held up a hand as Buck made to speak. 'OK, OK, we've come this far, I'll give it a shake for a little longer.'

'Much obliged.'

'So you goddamn should be.' Cole drew on his cheroot, then added, 'I can't believe they said that about me'

Buck smiled.

'Hard to believe, ain't it?' he agreed. And thought: maybe it's hard to believe because it never really happened. It was a straight-out lie. Buck Vallantry was no tinhorn. He knew he was likely facing up to more danger in the days ahead than he'd ever known existed. If that came to pass then he wanted this man he'd come to like and admire at his side. With his gun.

10

Singleman's Son

'Still here!' he said excitedly. 'Old friends — still here!'

The gunmen blinked at one another in astonishment as the overgrown boy went from one piece of equipment to another, touching them, fondling the couplings and cinches as though not prepared to accept the evidence of sight alone.

Between them, Holt and McClure couldn't recall ever having seen Singleman's son even mildly elated before, and hawk-faced Holt's service with the boss man dated back to before 'the event'.

Singleman senior insisted on referring to what had happened by that term, whereas what it had been in truth was nothing more than a violent man losing his temper at the wrong time.

David was fifteen at the time, a normal growing boy unaware as yet that his father was a Coloradan criminal only then just beginning to make his climb through semi-respectable political levels in Utah.

The game was handball and father and son were playing energetically against the rear wall of the big ranch house here in the Purple foothills, to which they'd now just returned after the years in the south. A normal game in every way other than that the boy for the very first time was beating the father. Singleman was not like other men. He couldn't take what was happening, and when they contested a vital point, both charging for the ball, he recklessly shouldered the boy from his path.

They were too close to the wall. David struck the wall with his head and had lain unconscious in the hospital for fifteen days before awakening with no memory of what had happened and an estimated sixty per cent impediment to the brain.

It was so long since they'd known David to remember anything that McClure, knowing just how the father would be pleased, ran up the broad steps and actually dared enter the conference room. Glasses resting on his imperious nose, Singleman looked up in annoyance. Seated around the huge circular table were army officers, bankers, speculators and any number of political figures with whom he had been associated during his climb to power in the county. This was the first full meeting since Singleman's whirlwind return and the only reason no Do Not Disturb sign had been hung on the doorknob was that nobody ever disturbed a conference.

'What the blue hell . . . ' Singleman began, but the excited guntipper spoke over him.

'Mr Singleman — David remembers his lifting gear!'

Singleman was on his feet in an instant as though the circle of important men did not exist. Guilt had been his constant companion ever since 'the event', even though he was a man who'd never experienced real guilt before.

The two went down the steps at the trot and crossed to the building housing the old weights. They found David heaving some impossible barbell over his head, still smiling as nobody remembered him doing before.

Singleman didn't remember quitting the room later. He'd never understood his ever-nagging guilt, but saw this as a sign that after all those years his son was at last on the way to recovery, perhaps might one day recover to such an extent that he might recall what had been done to him, and forgive.

It was the single sin in Singleman's lifelong litany of cruelties, injustices and reckless violences that actually seemed like a sin to him, and for which, for five long years, he'd secretly craved forgiveness.

This was a sign, he thought again, looking up at the great house and the powerful men gazing down at him, a signal that his return, already blessed with amazing success, would only grow greater. The future had never looked brighter and he could picture himself now, sharing it with his son.

★ ★ ★

From his small window in the sturdy stables, the colonel stared out at the scene before him — Singleman, the familiar figures of old foes lined up along the deep gallery, preening, the slouching gunmen with cigarettes in their mouths and servants bustling about their duties in the background.

Everything he saw, felt and heard proclaimed Singleman's total triumph, highlighting his own ultimate failure and inevitable death.

And yet the colonel stood ramrod erect, hands locked behind him, chin up and head back, the same deportment he'd exhibited every hour since the day of his capture. Enemies might justly accuse this vain and impressive man of many shortcomings, some of them more regrettable than others. But nobody could accuse the colonel of lacking courage, of steel in the sinews.

He didn't have to be told that with Singleman's return from the political wilderness already crowned with success, and his proud militia disbanded, he was of no possible further value to his abductor and could only pose a future danger to him should he be allowed to live.

But he would go like an officer and a man. That would be his final goal and one he knew he could achieve.

He raised his eyes to the brooding bulk of the Purple Mountains, which crowded Singleman's acres on the western side. So beautiful, so removed from all of man's ugly writhings and unworthy endeavours . . .

The colonel blinked and looked again. For one moment he was certain he'd caught a dim flash far up there, like sunlight winking off something

215

metallic such as a bridle bit, or perhaps a weapon . . .

It wasn't repeated and he guessed he was mistaken. He supposed it was time he stopped stargazing and completed what might well be the last loving letter to his daughter.

★   ★   ★

Enemy country. Danger country. Single-man country.

It stretched before them into the middle distance as the two men crouched deep in a nest of foothills boulders staring out over the fine grazelands in the direction they knew the headquarters were situated.

They looked for riders but didn't sight any. No cattle: they'd already established that fact coming down the mountainside. Nothing but gentle roll-ing hills down here, their own sweat-stained clothing, rasping breath.

And edginess.

'I must have been six kinds of a fool

to let you talk me into this,' Cole panted, pausing to sleeve his forehead. 'There has to be a better way, damnit. Look at it this way. Sooner or later Singleman will make a mistake, take his eye off the game, and then we move right in on him like the Rangers. But just two of us showing up right out here in the boondocks right at his goddamn fortress looks ... I must have been loco!'

'Ten thousand dollars,' Buck retorted. 'I've already told you, you can claim. I just want the colonel out of there alive, that's if he's still alive.'

'The goody-goody brother putting big bad brother in his place!' Cole sneered, sensing that the reason he was the edgy one here was because he'd seen far more gun action in his time than his brother, could assess more accurately exactly what they might find themselves up against down there. 'Don't you ever weary of that role?'

'You want to see the colonel walk out of here just as bad as I do, man.' Buck was equally exhausted by the mountain climb but was far calmer. 'I tell you if we keep our nerve and grab a little luck, we can reach the colonel before he gets murdered, and you can bag your catch. Easy money.'

Cole stared at his brother darkly. It was a long time since he'd last thought of his new-found kinsman as dumb or slow. Buck kept on proving himself, yet wasn't without his faults. Prime amongst these, Cole believed, was his need to prove himself a hero. Cole considered he was far beyond that small vanity himself. He was a veteran of the guns, not just a horse wrangler playing a danger game. He didn't crave accolades. He just wanted to be rich, and alive.

'It's not too late to change our — '

'We're not changing anything,' Buck cut him off. He pointed east. 'See that stand of pines on the knoll? We'll make it across to there and the rise should bring the headquarters in sight. We'll settle down and keep watch from there

218

until dark down, not far away now. Then we'll move in, following the attack plan we figured out on the way down.'

Cole shrugged.

'Sure, then it'll be simple. Two of the fearsome Vallantry boys up against a piddling — how many did we count from up there — ? Yeah, maybe up to an even dozen guntippers. A cinch.'

Buck studied his brother. He heard the sarcastic words but was seeing the face. Cole wasn't scared, it would have shown. It was his style to wrangle and disagree, like he was the only one capable of making plans, seeing a thing through.

'Sure it's going to be risky, Cole. But there's no guarantee we'll be going in after the colonel alone. Some of those militia old boys we talked to before we quit town seemed willing to ride out here after night-fall and join in — '

'And some sure as hell didn't.' Cole rose in a crouch. 'Do me a favor, just don't try and get me to see the bright side. Let's go.'

He was up and moving. Buck looked proud as he followed. Cole wasn't quitting. That was all that counted.

They made it to the knoll by which time the weak sun was resting on the western rim. The headquarters lay a mile distant. Men were moving about and a rider came in through the main gate from the south side. As they lay side by side beneath the pines they saw the first lights go on, rapidly strengthening as the dark came down.

'Know something, Buck?' The tone of Cole's voice had changed.

'What?'

'In case we don't both make it, I reckon you should know I wouldn't have missed this for, say, ten grand. Not the big chance of getting blown away out here in the boondocks, I don't mean that. But you know . . . this . . . the blood kin stuff and all . . . '

'Know what you mean and I feel the same. Let's go.'

They traveled swiftly, more running than walking, taking care where they placed their feet, all senses switched on and turned outwards. They crossed a burbling watercourse roughly halfway to their objective, bent even closer to the earth as they continued on. Deeper and deeper into Singleman territory, at its heart the citadel. Two men acting as one with their bridges burning behind them. Two men balancing upon the fulcrum of their lives — death if they failed or maybe achieving some state of grace should they succeed. Yet refusing now even to consider defeat. Brothers.

They were belly-wriggling through dew-damp grass by the time they reached the fence. The big house loomed. The citadel and center of it all. Silently they swigged from a canteen, exchanged a nod, slithered beneath the fence.

'What the hell was that?'

The voice came from so close by it couldn't help but startle. They pressed flat into the grass, eyes stabbing every which way. A sentry rose from behind a hay bale, light from the compound glinting on his carbine barrel. For a moment he seemed to be staring directly at them. Then he slowly turned away and Cole was up and upon him as swiftly as a canebreak panther. A dull thud, the man went down and Buck sprang erect.

'The back of the house and we'll work our way through from there!' he hissed and led the way forward at the run.

The sentry patrolling the gloomy house yard in back proved even easier pickings than the first. Cole flicked a pebble over his head and when the rifleman swung in that direction Buck cat-footed forward in a low crouch and brought him down with the butt of his .45.

Two down but how many to go? Only one way to find out.

They went up the rear steps and darted across the wide shadowed gallery. Dim light came from beneath a doorway. They'd glimpsed nothing untoward in the darkness, yet there seemed to be something in the air here, a vague stirring somewhere close by. With infinite caution, Cole eased a partly closed door open with the point of his sixshooter, couldn't suppress a gasp. Seated in a big chair beneath a low lamp, glass of whiskey in hand and a rifle carelessly in the other was a fierce-looking man with a black beard staring straight at them.

'Intruders!' he roared in a voice like a bullhorn and the brothers dropped flat and triggered back as the bellow of his gun shattered the night.

The gunman slumped sideways in the chair with a sudden hole where his right eye used to be. Above the reverberations of the gunfire came the voices, the shouting, the noise of alarm.

Then running footsteps.

'There's a staircase leading upstairs at the end of the porch,' Cole panted, leaping back through the door. 'Come on!'

They made it upstairs while clamor reigned below. Pounding along a narrow hallway they made it out to the front gallery, where two figures stood looking down.

The Vallantrys didn't hesitate. Not for a moment. Sixshooters raising an insane clatter, they pumped in shot after shot until one man crashed down on his face and a moment later his companion was slammed over the railing to plummet down onto the front steps like something that had never known life.

They were ahead, but for how long?

They'd counted upon stealth and rat cunning to get them farther than this, suddenly felt isolated up there on the upper floor with the rooms below rocking to the sounds of enraged shouting and pounding footsteps.

'There's only two of them, boss!' a hoarse voice bawled. 'I seen 'em goin' up the back stairs, two tall g — '

'Then get up there and bring them down in a sack!' cut in a voice laced with authority and thick with rage. 'All of you!'

So began the most desperate minutes of two men's lives as, darting from room to room and shooting at things they saw or only imagined they saw, each man took bullet grazes and accounted for two, maybe three more of the enemy in that savage slice of time. But it couldn't last and didn't. They were eventually forced back to the smoke-hazed front gallery from which there could be no possible retreat this time. Panting and leaking blood, they swiftly reloaded from their belts then stared silently at one another with the realization they'd lost.

No words. The moment was larger than that. A silent handclasp, then turning to face the hallway where the enemy was mustering his forces.

Then came the roaring volley that seemed to rock the night — yet not from close by. Not from the hallway or the house. Beyond.

Above the mounting crescendo of warring guns they detected the hammer of hoofbeats, glanced over the railing to stare down in disbelief. The homestead yard below was filled with horsemen pouring lead into the defenders on the lower gallery. Some of the riders sported hats turned up on one side exactly like those worn by the Free Citizens Militia!

They'd come!

A gun-toting figure came rushing from the upper hallway and both whirled and blasted him back the way he'd come. Then down the stairway with a great clatter of boots, the brothers shot their way through to the front in time to see the last of the defenders fling away their guns and raise their hands high.

Militiamen were already rushing this way and that in search of the colonel, while over by the barn a fierce scuffle was taking place.

Running in that direction, Buck and Cole realized that two militiamen had pinned an enraged Singleman's arms behind him and held him against a wall while another two were taking a fierce pounding by someone who kept saying, 'Bad men — David hurt. Bad men — David hurt.'

They were seeing Singleman's hugely muscled son for the first time but didn't know it.

'Leave him alone!' Singleman raged. Then, 'No, not the gunbutt! He's sick, he — '

Too late. The swinging rifle butt in the militiaman's hands slammed home with a sound like an axe biting wet wood. The blow might have killed a normal man but this man was far from that. David went down on one knee but his massive strength brought him to his feet with a dazed stare in his eyes, blinking like a man awakening from sleep.

It was a sleep of five years' duration, throughout which none of the endless line of high-priced physicians, whom the guilty Singleman had enlisted to treat his all but brain-dead son after his 'accident', had proven able to effect the slightest change in his condition.

It had taken the brutal smash of a rifle butt to the head to erase five years in the boy's injured brain and he was fifteen again and hurting.

'The ball!' he gasped. 'Where is the b — ?'

'David! Are you all right, son?'

Drawing closer now, the Vallantrys watched in amazement at the speed with which that great body turned, were close enough to see the sudden expression of terrible rage that contorted his features into a mask of animal hatred.

'You hurt me, father!'

It was the boy's voice, but a man's powerful body that lunged forward. The boy was flung back five years in time and the pain and disbelief of his father slamming him head-first into the wall of the handball court in an innocent game was primal, fearsome. For he was a man now and it was with a man's irresistible strength that David Singleman swept restraining militiamen away from his father then crashed a terrifying blow to the head.

'You hurt me, father!'

Singleman was on the ground as a size fourteen boot slammed into him, and the Vallantrys heard bones snap like sticks as each seized a mighty arm and heaved David against the wall.

He flung them away as though they were light-weights, lunging in to resume the attack as a bloody-faced Singleman got to his knees and raised both hands before him in a helpless gesture. A man got in the boy's path and was smashed aside like a child.

'Father is a bad man!'

It was Buck who tackled the powerful figure from behind, Cole who clamped a lock on one huge arm. But David was still struggling to his feet when quick-thinking militiamen hauled Singleman to his feet and began hauling him away from the danger.

'Bad man!' David shouted, his mighty rage slowly beginning to sub-side. He lurched to a halt with the brothers still pinning his arms.

'No, David, I love you!' Singleman cried, but the boy turned his back and Buck and Cole saw the father break apart before their eyes, no longer the man of power and cruelty, totally destroyed by the only one he'd ever loved, whose forgiveness he'd craved more than anything in life, now denied him forever.

Some of those watching almost felt sorry for Nick Singleman in that silent breaking moment. Almost.

★   ★   ★

'A good day for riding, brother.'

'Then ride, don't let me hold you back any. Brother.'

'Just thought you might've changed your mind, is all.'

'Why should I do that?'

'Well, the wild mustangs are still running in the high mesa country, for one. And two, you've got some reward ... Not as much as you figured, but ...sand ain't bad for a flash rooster of your tastes. You could maybe make that much again by the end of the season. With the mustangs.'

Leaning against a porch support of the General Store in Hopeville, Cole Vallantry was diverted momentarily by the clatter of hoofs and the goodbyes coming from the stage just rolling away from the depot opposite. The colonel and his daughter leaned from the windows and waved, neither appearing any the worse for wear after last night's celebrations, which were intended to lay all of Steuben County's troubles to rest and carry its people into the beckoning future.

As the coach rolled out, returning father and daughter to their much-interrupted vacation in the south, a totally calm looking David Singleman appeared on the porch of Doc Wilson's surgery along a couple of doors. Wilson's diagnosis tended to confirm the notion that the blow from the militiaman's rifle butt had reversed the damage the young man's brain had suffered at his father's hands. David's rage against his father out at the ranch had been for the boy as though the intervening years had never happened.

Doc had proclaimed that, as far as he could determine, the boy was fully recovered to the level he had been before the injury and in his opinion should be quite capable of living a normal life.

Buck swung up and settled into his saddle.

'Last chance, high-stepper. Clean living, fast horses, good times and easy money to be made on one hand, or dingy saloons, cheap women and most likely some backshooter waiting for you behind the next stacked deck you ring in on the other. What's it to be?'

He sounded off-handed but was far from it. But whichever way the cards fell, Buck Vallantry was riding south.

'Always knew you were a hick,' came the reply. 'Together, we could make more next week than you'll make in a year with the broomtails.'

Buck just nodded and eased his heavily laden mount into a walk. The Sioux stallion snorted and shook its head, eager for the trails. Folks along the street waved him off as he made it to the first cross-street and turned down it. He kept his horse to a walk until clear of the last house then lifted it to a lope. He covered two miles before he hipped around in the saddle to look back, grinned.

A solitary horseman was riding out of town behind him.

THE END